by Sarah Willson

SCHOLASTIC INC.

New York   Toronto   London   Auckland   Sydney
Mexico City   New Delhi   Hong Kong

Based on the TV series *Rugrats®* created by Arlene Klasky, Gabor Csupo,
and Paul Germain as seen on Nickelodeon®

ISBN 0-439-25965-7

12 11 10 9 8 7 6 5 4 3 2   2 3 4 5/0

Printed in the U.S.A.

First Scholastic printing, February 2001

CHAPTER 1

"Hey! Where did my sand pail go?" asked Tommy Pickles. He and Chuckie and Phil and Lil and Angelica were playing in the sandbox in the Pickleses' backyard. Tommy's parents had taken his baby brother, Dil, to the doctor for a checkup.

"What sand pail, Tommy?" asked Chuckie.

"My blue one," Tommy replied, still searching for it. "The one that Spike chewed. I've had it ever since I was little." Tommy peered outside the sandbox, looking in all directions.

His cousin Angelica was playing with her Superstar Cynthia doll at the far end of the sandbox. Nearby, Grandpa Lou lay on his lawn chair, examining some vacation brochures. Angelica snorted. "Oh, brother. Why would anyone care about a stupid holey pail, anyway?"

"Eh? What's that?" said Grandpa Lou, suddenly looking up. He wasn't wearing his hearing aid. "Holy Grail? Holy Toledo! I haven't thought about the Holy Grail since I was just a spud!" Grandpa Lou got a faraway look in his eyes. "My granddaddy used to read me the story of King Arthur and his knights of the Round Table and their search for the Holy Grail."

"What is the Holey Pail, anyway?" Angelica asked in a louder voice. "And why were knightses playing at a sand table?"

"Lands, what *do* they teach you in school these days?" Grandpa exclaimed.

"But, Grandpa, we don't go to school yet. And I said pail. Holey *pail*," Angelica shouted.

But Grandpa didn't hear her. He was already off and running with his story. "Why, the Holy Grail was a sacred container that was supposed to reveal the Secret of Life. The knights of the Round Table spent a heap of time searching for it, but only a couple of 'em ever actually caught a glimpse of it." Grandpa looked at Angelica and the babies.

The babies stared blankly back at him.

He shook his head in amazement. "You mean to tell me you kids don't know the legend of King Arthur? Why, when I was a young'un, we spent our time reading books, not watching that nonsense you kids watch on TV all day. I used to walk FIFTEEN miles to the library once a week, take out FIFTEEN books, and read 'em all in FIFTEEN minutes. Yes sirree, and the King Arthur legends were my favorites." Grandpa Lou patted his lawn chair. "Come on over here, kids, and I'll tell you all about them."

Angelica and the babies clambered out of the sandbox and over to Lou. They climbed onto the lawn chair and snuggled up against him.

"A long time ago," he began, "even before my great-great-great-granddaddy was born, there lived a great king named Arthur, who ruled over the kingdom of Camelot."

"Uh, Grandpa?" Angelica said, tugging his sleeve. "I hate to interrupt your story, but why is it getting dark out here? It isn't even lunchtime yet!"

Grandpa Lou looked up at the sky. There wasn't a cloud in it. "I was just wondering that same thing myself," he said, puzzled. "I thought my spectacles were acting up on me again."

In a few minutes it was nearly pitch-black. Chuckie began to chew on his shirt. Phil and Lil clutched each other tightly. Tommy snuggled closer to his Grandpa.

"Cynthia! Where are you?" wailed Angelica. "I must have left her in the sandbox!"

"What in tarnation!" exclaimed Grandpa's voice in the blackness. "This must be a total eclipse of the sun!"

"A totally flipped sun?" exclaimed Angelica.

"An eclipse!" said Grandpa Lou. "Whatever you kids do, don't look right at it or you could hurt your eyes. An eclipse is when the moon passes right in front of the sun, making it get dark on some parts of the earth. Some folks believe that eclipses cause all sorts of strange shenanigans to happen. 'Course it's all hogwash."

While Grandpa Lou was talking, the sky had begun to grow lighter. In a few moments the sun was shining brightly again. Everyone blinked and looked around.

"Uh, Grandpa?" Angelica said in a tiny voice. "Where did the sandbox go? And where's Aunt Didi and Uncle Stu's house?"

The babies looked around. Chuckie was so shocked, he tumbled off the lawn chair and onto the soft, muddy grass. Grandpa Lou took off his glasses, polished them on his shirt, put them back on again, and looked around. The sandbox and house had indeed disappeared. In their place was a rolling green meadow. Next to the lawn chair grew a large, shady tree whose leafy branches swayed gently in the soft breeze. Lambs dotted the hillside. And in the distance they could make out a town surrounded by high stone walls. On the hill in the center-most part of the town stood a magnificent castle. Flags bearing gold lions against deep red backgrounds fluttered from the castle's many towers.

"Heavens to Gimbel's, I must have nodded off!" Grandpa exclaimed. "I'm dreaming we're all in Camelot. I *thought* my iced tea tasted a little funny at the Lodge this morning!" He settled back in the lawn chair and looked around dreamily. "Maybe if I lie here really still, the dream will keep on going for a little while longer." Several moments went by. Angelica and the babies sat speechless with surprise. After a few more moments, Grandpa Lou yawned. His eyes began to droop.

"Tommy?" whispered Chuckie. "Tommy, where are we?"

"I'm not sure, Chuckie," said Tommy. "But it doesn't look like my backyard, does it?"

"Um, no."

"I don't 'member seeing that big gray house before," said Lil, pointing toward the huge castle.

"I don't, either," said Phil.

"Who cares about big gray houses? Where's Cynthia?" cried Angelica, jumping to her feet.

Grandpa Lou began to snore softly. And then they heard a sound approaching. It was a *cloppety-clopping* from somewhere behind the tree, accompanied by what sounded like the *clankety-clanking* of pots and pans. The sound grew closer and closer, and then stopped. Tommy looked up and found himself staring at three horses standing very still and looking down at him. Two were white, and the third was a glossy black. The backs of the horses were draped with bright-colored, fringed banners. Long, plumed feathers adorned their heads.

Tommy's gaze moved upward, toward the three figures sitting on the backs of the three horses. Each wore a curious sort of metal body-suit that looked as though it were made of swing set chains all linked together. Even their hands and feet were covered with the stuff. It appeared to be somewhat uncomfortable to wear. Tommy noticed one of the riders trying in vain to scratch his own elbow.

"Confounded chain mail," the rider muttered to himself.

Over the chain mail each rider wore a long, sleeveless shirt, belted at the waist. One was made of black velvet. Another was of gold satin. The third was red linen. The shields the riders carried bore different symbols: One had a lion, the next a dragon, and the third a curly letter "B."

Each rider wore what looked like a metal

bucket on his head, with just a few small holes punched out for seeing and breathing.

"Tommy," whispered Chuckie, "why do those guys have garbage cans on their heads?"

"And stretchy shirts made out of metal?" added Lil.

Phil nudged his sister and pointed toward the riders' long swords. "I don't think those are toy swordses," he whispered.

Angelica stood up and faced the riders, her hands on her hips and her head tilted to one side. "Are you real knightses?" she demanded to know.

None of the three responded, except to move their hands onto their swords and to sit up straighter. Finally the black knight pulled the metal bucket off his head and tucked it under one arm. He peered closely down at them. "By the rood, are these Saxon spies disguised as children?" he asked. He was clean-shaven, with reddish hair. Perspiration had plastered his thick bangs to his forehead. The rest of his hair was cropped straight across just below his ears.

The other two knights took off their headgear to get a better look at the babies. The gold knight had a thick black mustache that curled up at the ends, and a pointy beard at the tip of his chin. A gold banner flapped from his long, deadly lance. The red knight had blond hair nearly down to his shoulders.

"Perhaps the gray-haired one is under a spell," mused the gold knight, pointing at Grandpa Lou, whose head had rolled back and whose mouth had come open. "He sleepeth, yet it is not even noontime."

"He always sleepeth," Angelica explained. Then she looked closely at something in the red knight's hand. "Hey! Where'd you find my Cynthia doll?" she asked.

The other babies looked where she was pointing. Sure enough, the red knight clasped Angelica's doll in his gloved hand.

The knight raised the doll before his eyes. "As my name is Sir Casey de Batt, this is truly a wondrous statue," he said. "Her features are perfect, her figure sublime, her dress festooned with flowers and made from a material I have never before seen."

11

"Well, right!" said Angelica. "That's a dress from the all-new Superstar Cynthia Cruise Wear Collection! My mom just bought it for me! So give her back, please!"

The knight continued as though he hadn't heard a word Angelica had just said. "I found her in the sandpit over there. It is clearly a sign that she belongs with us. As we are on our way to strange parts, to join the search for the Holy Grail, we shall carry this statue with us as our mistress and our guiding beacon. She will guide us in case we should encounter unforeseen dangers."

"You mean," said Angelica, her voice rising shrilly, "you want to take her with you when you go look for the Holey Pail? But she's mine!" Angelica stomped her foot.

The knight holding the doll turned to address the black knight. "Sir Boyle Enoil," he said, "as we are in a hurry, methinks it would be wise to send these strangers back to Camelot with our squires."

"'Tis well thought, Sir Casey," Sir Boyle replied. With that he put two fingers in his mouth and whistled such a piercing sound that the birds ceased to twitter for a moment. It woke Grandpa Lou with a start and he sat up, looking around in confusion.

A moment later a group of riders thundered over the slope and came to a halt so quickly, one or two nearly flew over the front of their horses. Then an empty cart clattered up, pulled by two more horses.

"Take these babes and their smooth-headed caregiver back to Camelot, to be presented before the king," said Sir Casey to the horsemen.

The babies and Angelica were scooped up and set into the cart. Grandpa was boosted up onto a horse. The three knights gave their horses' reins a shake and began to trot away in the opposite direction.

"Hey!" Angelica yelled over her shoulder at the retreating knights. "You bring me back my doll! You can't go taking dolls away from little girls! Whatever happened to the days of shovelry, anyway?"

"Where are the knightses going?" asked Lil.

"They're going to look for a holey pail," replied Phil.

13

"You mean there's just one pail and they all gotta share it?" asked Lil.

"I guess so," said Tommy. "I hope they find it soon, 'cause those metal stretchies they got on don't look very comfortable."

"This is some dream!" Grandpa said to himself as his horse turned around to face Camelot. "Never felt so real before!"

Still fuming, Angelica watched the knights disappear, carrying Cynthia with them. And then she and Grandpa and the babies were taken away in the direction of the castle.

CHAPTER 2

"Where are they taking us, Tommy?" whispered Chuckie as the wall surrounding the castle in the distance grew larger and larger.

"I think we're going to see King Arthur and the knightses of the Sand Table," Tommy whispered back.

"Good," said Angelica. "I'm going straight to the top! I've got a thing or two to tell that king about how his knightses go around stealin' dolls from adorable little girls."

The cart and horses clattered onto an uneven, cobbled street and through a huge, stone archway. Then they began climbing a steep hill that wound its way up toward the center of the town. Above them loomed the castle, its gray towers and battlements draped with ivy, its bright-colored flags flapping briskly in the breeze. Along the way people stopped to stare at the procession. Tommy noticed that most of them were dressed in clothing made out of coarse brown cloth. Some wore sandals; others were barefoot. A few children ran alongside their cart as it rolled up the hill.

"Where are we?" Tommy called to a little boy.

"Camelot!" the little boy called back.

"*Camel* Lot?" Tommy said, turning to Chuckie.

"I thought camels were only in the desert," Chuckie replied.

"Guess not."

At last they reached the castle. The drawbridge was lowered down for them with a loud creak.

"Are there alligators in there, Tommy?" asked Chuckie, peering into the green water.

"Um, no, Chuckie, I'm sure this is just a goldfishy pond they use for decreation," Tommy said, reassuring him.

"Can we go swimming?" asked Phil.

Just then a rider ahead of them casually

threw the remains of a chicken drumstick into the moat. The water immediately boiled up with churning white bubbles. When the bone floated back to the surface, it was picked clean.

"I don't think I like those goldfishies, Tommy," said Chuckie.

Once across the drawbridge, the riders dismounted and led the horses into the castle courtyard. They helped Grandpa Lou down, then picked up the babies. Angelica leaped out of the cart. Servants appeared out of nowhere to lead the horses away. Then Tommy and the others were brought into the main entrance hall of the castle. It was dark and gloomy, even though the sun had been shining brightly outside. The only windows were very small, and high above their heads. Torches flickered, and rich tapestries covered the stone walls. A fireplace, large enough to ride a horse into without bumping its rider's head, took up one end of the hall.

"Pray summon us before His Majesty," the head squire said to one of the servants, who immediately hurried away.

He was back a moment later. "My liege, the king bids you enter."

"No one pinch me!" said Grandpa Lou with a big grin on his face. "I want to keep dreaming long enough to see King Arthur and the knights of the Round Table!"

Once inside, they saw a huge round table that took up most of the enormous room. About one hundred knights sat around it, each in full chain mail and bright-colored tunics.

The table was fashioned into a doughnut shape, with the center part cut away. A hinged section could be lifted up so subjects could be brought to stand inside it. The section was lifted, and a servant led Grandpa and the babies inside the circle, where they found themselves being stared at by a hundred pairs of curious eyes.

There was no mistaking which one was the king. King Arthur sat directly in front of them, his gold throne inlaid with precious jewels, a circlet of jeweled gold around his head. His hair and beard were gold, and his white tunic had a shimmering red dragon on it. The chair to his right was empty. In the chair to his left sat a beautiful woman who could only be the queen.

"Hot dog!" exclaimed Grandpa, looking around excitedly. "I'll betcha that's Arthur, and that guy over there is Sir Lancelot, and that fella there could be Gawain, or possibly Gareth? And, of course, that's Queen Guinevere. She looks every bit the knockout I imagined she would, which makes sense, of course, 'cause this is all my imagination."

"Enough with thy endless prattle, O Aged One," whispered the servant who had brought them into the circle. "I must announce thee to our king." Then he cleared his throat importantly, took a deep breath, and spoke in a booming voice: "His Majesty, King Arthur, son of Uther Pendragon, defeater of Saxons and king of the Britons, behold the Aged One and these babes, heroically apprehended in the royal pastures by the Grail-seeking knights Sir Casey, Sir Boyle, and Sir Gnatt and sent to His Majesty with their compliments!" The servant gasped for air, having uttered his speech in one breath.

King Arthur stood up and looked curiously at Grandpa and the rest of the group.

Grandpa still had a delighted look on his face. He marched over to the king and leaned across the table. Grandpa grasped the king's hand and shook it warmly. The crowd of knights and servants gasped out loud. Even Guinevere looked shocked, but she reached up and closed her ruby-red mouth with a lily-white hand.

"So glad to meetcha!" said Grandpa Lou to the king, who appeared to be struck dumb with astonishment.

"Has he lost his mind?" murmured a knight who was sitting near Tommy. "To treat the king so familiarly is asking for his head to be removed from his shoulders!"

"Perhaps he is a powerful sorcerer," whispered another knight. "Why else would he treat the king as an equal?"

"Mayhap he is the great magician, Merlin, returned to Camelot in disguise?" said a third.

Arthur must have been thinking along the same lines, for he asked Grandpa: "Are you a great and powerful sorcerer? I have never before seen such a wondrous creation as that which sits upon your nose." He pointed to Grandpa's glasses.

"What, my spectacles?" said Grandpa, taking them off and holding them in front of him.

The king must have thought Grandpa was giving them to him as a gift, for he took them out of Grandpa's hands and placed them on his own nose. A slow smile spread across the king's face as he gazed around the room. "Why, Lancelot!" he said, turning toward a stately knight dressed head to toe in chain mail. "I have never before noticed how your nose dominates your face quite so!"

A knight a few chairs down from Arthur blushed and covered his nose with his hand.

"And Sir Gareth, I did not notice before this moment how like a weasel your face appears!"

A knight in a green tunic with a large yellow "G" ducked quickly below the table, as though looking for something.

"I can't see a cotton-pickin' thing without my glasses," said Grandpa, but King Arthur was too busy looking around in wonder. Beside him, the queen stood up from her gilded throne.

"What curious costumes!" said Queen Guinevere, stepping down from her gilded throne and peering across the table at Grandpa's rumply shirt. The words VIVA LAS VEGAS! were written across it. "Is that a Latin quotation? I know not what it means."

"Pardon me, Your Majesty," interrupted a servant. "In searching the strangers for weapons, we came upon these in the old one's pocket." He handed the king some glossy materials.

"Oh, hey!" said Grandpa. "Those are my vacation brochures! I still haven't decided between Las Vegas and Atlantic City!"

King Arthur peered through Grandpa's glasses at one of the brochures, and handed the other to the queen. "I have never heard of these faraway kingdoms." He glanced down at the brochure again. "But look at these paintings! They seem so clear, the colors so true!" He was staring at a photograph of a glittery Las Vegas hotel.

"That's the Knight-Life Hotel and Casino," said Grandpa. "It's got ten roulette wheels and a thousand slot machines! And the dealers dress like knights and damsels. Hmmm. Maybe I should do that one after all."

Arthur was impressed. He looked up at Grandpa, "Thou must be a wealthy man to be able to fashion such marvelous documents as these," he said as he held up the brochure. "And your weavers are very skilled," he said, pointing toward Lou's shirt with a jeweled hand. "And your powers of sorcery must be strong indeed to help the eye see so clearly." He pointed to the glasses on his own nose. "Welcome, sir. We are honored to have such a great sorcerer to Camelot."

"But who are these children?" asked Queen Guinevere, looking down at Angelica and the babies.

"I'm glad you finally noticed me!" chimed in Angelica. "Because I need to have a word with you about one of the knightses from the sand table, who took a certain doll—"

The queen, who seemed preoccupied by Lou's attire, clapped her hands, and a group of servants appeared instantly. "Take these babies to the royal nursery!" The servants picked up Tommy, Chuckie, Phil, and Lil and politely guided Angelica toward the door.

"Stay, sir," said Queen Guinevere to Grandpa, who had turned to follow the children out of the Round Table room. "They shall be well looked after. I beg you to reveal the magic of thy dentistry!" She pointed at Grandpa's mouth. "How could your smile be so white, and yet you be so advanced in years?"

"What, these?" said Grandpa, popping out his dentures. He seemed pleased she had noticed. "Beft teef mummy cam buy!"

Grandpa started to chatter away about his false teeth to various members of the court, who examined them with keen interest, while the babies were escorted out of the room.

The royal nursery was a few flights up a winding stone staircase. Inside, it looked like the other rooms Tommy had seen of the castle: but scattered about the place were objects resembling toys, though they were unlike any toys the babies had seen before. Stone blocks were strewn around one end of the room. A wooden bowl was filled with what appeared to be bleached-white chicken bones. There were some crude dolls with painted faces, some handmade rattles, a drum, and some large hoops made out of green branches.

Sitting at the far end of the room, just below where the window shed a faint light on her needlepoint, sat a large, kindly looking woman, who dozed softly in her chair.

There were three babies at play, as well as one older boy who looked about Angelica's age. The servants deposited Tommy and the others on the floor of the nursery and hurried away. The three babies approached Tommy and his friends curiously. They all wore white cotton playsuits with lots of frilly white lace down the front. A little girl with golden curls, who seemed to be about Chuckie's age, was the first to speak.

"Who are you?" she asked. "I'm Adelaide, but you can call me Addy. And this is Percivale, and that's Galahad." She gestured to the two babies standing next to her. "And that kid over there," she said, rolling her eyes a little, "that's Mordred. He doesn't like to play with us."

"How come?" asked Phil curiously.

"He says he's stuperior to us, which really isn't true, since all *our* dads are knightses. Oh, and *his* mom is a witch. She drops him off so she can spend her time casting evil spells on people. The king invites them to the castle a lot."

"Why?" asked Chuckie.

"Because she's got him bewitched. The king still hasn't realized that Mordred's mom wants to take over Camelot."

Mordred appeared to be ignoring the newcomers. He was busying himself across the room, tearing the arms off a couple of dolls.

Tommy smiled at Adelaide. "I'm Tommy, and this is Chuckie and Phil and Lil. Angelica here's my cousin."

"Okay, okay," said Angelica. "Let's cut the nicey talk. These are the weirdest-looking toys I ever saw. Don't you have any Superstar Cynthia stuff? What do you guys do for fun around here?"

"Well," said Adelaide thoughtfully, "we can show you a trapdoor over there that we found. It leads to a slide that goes right downstairs. When our nanny falls asleep, we sometimes leave the nursery to go explore the castle." She sighed. "But these days I don't really feel like doing much exploring or anything."

"How come?" asked Tommy.

She sighed again. "My dad is missing."

Chuckie's eyes widened. "Did he get lost at the mall or something?" he said.

"No. He was on a quest for the Holy Grail."

"Why does he want a holey pail so bad?" Lil asked. "They leak, you know."

"No, no," said Adelaide, "I'm talking about the Holy Grail—-that fancy container that's really famous. Everyone is always looking for it, but no one ever finds it. What usually happens is, knightses go out searching for it and then they don't come back, so then the king sends out search parties to go search for the knightses. Well, they sent a search party out for my dad and the other knightses he was with, but now *that* search party hasn't come back, either. So

King Arthur is getting really worried, because my dad is one of his bestest knightses. You've probably heard of him. Sir Nedd of Nutt?"

The babies shook their heads politely "no."

"No? Well, anyway, he's been gone a long time, and I'm worried." She sighed again. "And now the king is missing at least twelve knightses from his Table, and he's getting worried that something really bad has happened to them." She turned to look over at Mordred, and her eyes narrowed. "I gotta funny feeling that Mordred and his mom might know something about all this. Did I mention that Mordred's mother is a witch?"

"Yes, you did. Twice already," snapped Angelica. "I wonder if those three knightses we saw in the sheep meadow were going out searching for your dad," she mused. Her face darkened. "They're the ones who took my doll! If they're missing now, then that means that Cynthia must be missing too!"

Mordred had come over by this time and was eyeing them with obvious dislike. "Where'd you babies come from, anyway?" he asked.

"Tommy's sandbox," Lil answered.

Mordred didn't appear to be particularly interested in her answer. Instead, he said, "I hope you're not staying long."

Galahad rolled his eyes. "Mordred, just because your mom is the meanest witch in the kingdom doesn't give you the right to be mean too."

"Yeah," said Angelica. "If anyone gets to be mean to these four babies right here, it's gonna be me!"

Mordred crossed his arms and tried to look tough, but he was not much taller than Chuckie. "I think you babies better go back where you came from. I wouldn't want anything bad to happen to you." He grinned in a way that Tommy didn't like.

Adelaide rolled her eyes. "Mordred, why don't you go change yourself into a bug or something," she said.

Suddenly trumpets sounded, and the doors to the nursery were flung open. The woman with the needlepoint opened her eyes and quickly jumped to her feet.

"The king requests these babes be brought before him once again!" a servant called to her.

The servants quickly picked up the babies and took Angelica by the hand. "Great," muttered Angelica. "Maybe it's finally time for lunch. I hope the food around here is better than the toys," she grumbled as they walked out of the room.

CHAPTER 3

As Angelica and the babies were brought into the Round Table room, a lovely maiden was speaking to the king. The knights of the Round Table gazed at her as she spoke.

The maiden held something draped across her arms. It was a beautiful cloak. It shimmered with gold and silver threads, and was studded with hundreds of precious gems.

"Your Majesty, my mistress, Morgan le Fay, sends this gift with her compliments," said the maiden in a lilting, beautiful voice. "She asked me to place it personally upon Your Majesty's shoulders, that all may see the richness of its workmanship."

Arthur was looking pleased. He was standing directly in front of the maiden, inside the Round Table, and he took a step forward to allow her to place it around him.

Angelica gave a loud snort.

The king stopped, startled, and looked at her.

"That looks like a *girl's* cape, if you ask me," Angelica said.

The maiden turned toward Angelica with a nasty expression on her face.

"You think so?" asked Arthur in a worried tone.

"Well, don't get me wrong," said Angelica. "It's a nice-looking dress and all, but I'm not sure it suits a tough-guy king like you."

Arthur studied the cloak for a moment, then spoke directly to the maiden. "Let's try this on your own shoulders, so that we may better see whether it flatters you or me."

All the color left the maiden's face. She started to stammer, then began edging away. Arthur's face began to cloud with suspicion. "I command thee!" he thundered.

With trembling hands the maiden threw the cloak around her own shoulders. For a moment nothing happened. Then, right before everyone's eyes, she began to shrink. Her hands touched the floor so that she was on all fours. Her nose grew broader, her eyes moved toward the outside of her face, her ears lengthened, and her clothes disappeared. She had turned into a pig! With a loud squeal and several snorts, the pig dashed from the room.

A hush fell. And then Sir Lancelot cried, "There is dirty work afoot! The cloak made for the king by the evil witch Morgan le Fay has changed the false maiden into a pig! The child Angelica has saved the king's life!"

"Could this child be a sorceress like her grandfather?" cried Sir Gawain.

"Huh?" said Angelica. "Oh! Yeah! I could! I *am* a sorcer-less!"

The babies stared at her in surprise.

Every knight in the place bowed down low. Angelica smiled her most angelic smile.

"I am grateful to you for my life," Arthur said to her. "Speak, child sorceress, and I shall grant you anything you desire, even if it be half my kingdom."

Tommy could practically hear the wheels

grinding in Angelica's head. "Well first of all, Your Majesty, you know Sir Casey? One of the knightses of your sand table? He took my Cynthia doll. So, could you find him, please, and make him give her back?"

"But he has vanished like a raindrop on the surface of a pond. No man can find him."

"All right, I guess I'll have to go find Cynthia myself," said Angelica. "But in the meantime, do you have any pizza? I'm starved! Oh, and cookies would be nice too."

Arthur clapped his hands twice, and instantly the royal chef appeared. "I command thee to make this child and her friends . . . *peas-uh* and *cookeries!*" the king said, looking in Angelica's direction.

The chef began to tremble violently. His hands flew to his neck, as though he was already anticipating being sent to the block. Then he started to babble. "Your Majesty, I know not the secret of how to make these noble dishes—"

"Don't worry, I'll show ya," Angelica said ˈ ˈ rfully, and she led the chef from the room.

Over her shoulder she called back casually to the king, "Oh, and a swimming pool in the castle courtyard would be great."

"It shall be done!" Arthur called after her.

As the babies were carried back to the nursery, they passed a room where Grandpa Lou sat with Guinevere, flanked by a dozen beautiful ladies of the court. He was teaching them to play cards. The queen was speaking to him: "And I shall have playing cards created with My Lord as the king, and Sir Lancelot as the jack! But what meaneth thee by 'a royal flush'?"

Back in the nursery, the babies found Galahad, Adelaide, and Percivale. Mordred was not there.

"His mom sent her servant to come pick him up," Galahad explained. "She heard about how you saved the king from her spell, so she wanted to get Mordred out of here."

"You mean, Mordred's mom is that Morgan le Fay?" asked Tommy, wide-eyed.

"Mmm-hmm," replied Galahad. "Morgan le Fay has been trying to get rid of the king for years now. For a while there, she acted like she wanted to be his friend, but lately she's been acting meaner and meaner to him. After the cloak thing, I think the king will finally figure out that she isn't as nice as he thought she was."

"Why does she want to get rid of the king?" asked Lil.

"So she can be the ruler of Camelot," Galahad replied. "She's been rounding up armies from other countries to come fight him, like Saxons and Normans, but so far, the Knightses of the Round Table have been able to make them all go away. But now that all these knightses have started to disappear, King Arthur's Round Table is getting weaker. We think Morgan's got something to do with all the missing knightses."

"And now Mordred is really jealous of Angelica because he thinks she's got stronger magical powers than he does. He can still only do little baby spells," Percivale added.

"And Morgan is worried because she thinks your grandpa is really powerful too. She thinks he's here to protect the king. I heard the king wants to have new teeth made just like your grandpa's," said Adelaide.

"Yeah, the king only has a few teeth," said Phil.

"I know. I have more than he does," said Lil.

Adelaide sighed. "I wish my dad had been here to see Angelica save the king's life."

"Don't worry, Addy," Tommy soothed her. "We're gonna help you find your dad, aren't we, guys?"

"We are?" asked Chuckie. Then he watched as Adelaide shook away a golden curl to wipe a tear from her eye. "Yes. We *are* going to find him!" he declared.

CHAPTER 4

"I tell ya, this is the life—huh, guys?" Angelica said to the babies as she popped another peeled grape into her mouth. "A girl could get used to being treated like a sorcer-less!"

Tommy, Chuckie, Phil, and Lil were splashing happily in the pool that had been built for them. It was a large, shallow, kidney-shaped structure, built of smooth marble and filled with cool green water. Scented lily pads floated on the surface. Servants stood by at a respectful distance, waiting to refill the babies' golden sippy cups and bottles with warm milk.

Chuckie stepped out of the pool and padded over to a velvet chair. "I just can't help thinking about poor Addy's dad, Sir Nedd," he said. "I wonder what happened to him."

A servant appeared carrying a steaming

platter of cookies. Bowing low, he set it down and then backed away from them.

Angelica rang a little bell next to her lounge chair. Two knights entered the courtyard in full armor. One wore a long green tunic, another a long red tunic. They clattered over to where Angelica sat.

"Let's play Red Knight, Green Knight again!" Angelica said, jumping up.

The red knight drooped in his armor. "Again?" he said, groaning. "Maybe you can play a different knightly game for a while, as we are worn out. It is not easy to run in this stuff," he said peevishly, plucking at his heavy chain mail.

"Oh, all right," Angelica said crossly, and she pulled a gold rope. A curtain opened at one end of the courtyard, revealing an archway into another yard where some knights were playing basketball.

"'Tis a foul!" cried one knight.

"What didst thou say?" yelled his opponent, aghast.

"Thou heardst me! Thou didst strike me upon the arm!"

The knight who had been accused of fouling took off his glove and threw it on the ground at his opponent's feet.

Angelica sighed. She didn't like watching that sport anymore, either. She pulled the curtain closed again. "It's boring playing with knightses. And they're getting fat, eating all that pizza." She sighed. "I just can't enjoy the good life without Cynthia."

Tommy jumped up. "Angelica and Chuckie are right. I can't stand thinking about how Addy's daddy needs help while we lie around here all day, swimmin' and playin' with toys and enjoying the good life. Let's leave the Camel Lot and go search for Addy's daddy and the other missing knightses."

"Okay, and when we find those knightses, I'm going to make them give Superstar Cynthia a horse to ride all for herself!" Angelica said, also jumping out of her chair.

Chuckie gulped. "On second thought, they'll probably be back any day now. Let's just stay here and wait for them. Who knows what's out there, beyond the castle walls?"

"But, Chuckie, I think something's happened to them!" said Tommy. "We gots to go save them!"

"What about your grandpa, Tommy?" asked Lil. "Should we take him with us?"

"Yes. We can't leave him by himself," Tommy said firmly. "He needs us to take care of him."

"I'll get the royal chef to pack us up a whole bunch of food," Angelica said smugly. "He does whatever I tell him to, so I'll make sure it's mostly cakes and cookies."

"Let's get going," said Tommy.

CHAPTER 5

The next morning Grandpa Lou and the babies got ready to set off on their quest. A large cart had been prepared for them, pulled by two donkeys. Grandpa Lou held the reins. The cart was piled high with food and diapers. Tied behind it was a large cow, which Queen Guinevere had ordered for their journey so as to keep the babies supplied with fresh milk.

The babies from the nursery had come to see them off. "Thanks a lot, you guys," Adelaide whispered to her new friends as she stood on tiptoe and peered into the cart. "I wish I could come with you, but I got to stay behind and take care of my mom."

"Don't worry, Addy," Chuckie whispered back. "We'll find your dad."

Addy placed something gently into

Chuckie's hand. It was a small portrait of herself in a fancy gold frame. "Take this," she whispered. "For good luck." Then she rummaged around in the folds of her dress and pulled out a second item. "Oh, and take this, too. It's my trusty squirt gun. You might need it."

Chuckie blushed and shoved both items into his pocket.

King Arthur had come outside to bid them good-bye. He was still wearing Grandpa's glasses. "We pray you make haste," Arthur said to Grandpa Lou. "With your powerful magic, and yours"—he looked at Angelica—"I am certain you will find the missing knights and bring them back here to my Round Table. You shall restore the court of Camelot to its former glory!"

"Eh?" said Grandpa, who could neither hear without his hearing aid nor see without his glasses. "Right! I'm sure a picnic in the country will be just the ticket on a gorgeous day like today! We'll see you this afternoon!"

With a puzzled look on his face, Arthur waved good-bye, and the cart creaked away.

Before they had even gotten to the top of the first hill, Grandpa Lou stretched. "Guess I'll catch a little shut-eye," he said yawning. "I just hope I don't wake up from the dream!" And with that, he fell fast asleep.

They traveled through beautiful green countrysides, up gently rolling hills, and past rustic stone walls. "I gotta idea," said Tommy.

"What kind of idea, Tommy?" Chuckie asked, looking warily at his friend.

"I think I know where we should look first for Addy's daddy," Tommy replied.

"How come I gotta funny feeling I'm not going to like your idea?" Chuckie said.

"I think the first place we should try is Morgan le Fay's castle," Tommy said.

"Are you nuts?" said Angelica. "She'll turn us into frogs and throw us right into her moat or something!"

"Yeah, I gots a better idea," said Chuckie. "Let's find out where her castle is and go the opposite dissection!"

"But Chuckie, remember we're trying to save Addy's daddy, right?" said Lil.

"And the other knightses of the Sand Table," added Phil.

"And, Angelica," said Tommy, "remember who else is probably at Morgan's castle: Cynthia!"

That hit home. Angelica looked horrified, and then her eyes narrowed. "Okay, you're right. For once. Let's go to Morgan's castle and show her and her son Mordred a thing or two!"

"But, Tommy, how do we know where it is?" asked Lil.

"Look," Tommy said, pointing.

Far off on the horizon they could see a gray area in the sky. Everywhere else it was clear, blue, and sunny. The gray area was made of dark, heavy clouds. The clouds hovered directly over a tall castle.

The closer the cart got, the more details the babies were able to make out.

"Are those bats flying around that house?" Phil wanted to know.

"It looks like it," said Tommy. "I bet that's Morgan's castle."

Chuckie gave a tiny squeak. "It looks like it's

raining over there, but it's not raining any-where else."

They continued in silence for a while, except for Grandpa Lou's gentle snores.

The cart reached the bottom of a long, steep hill. They couldn't see the castle from the bot-tom, but they could see the gray clouds. A light rain began to fall. It grew steadier and steadier.

Finally, Grandpa Lou woke up. "What? Where am I?" he asked groggily. He looked down at the babies and Angelica.

"We're climbing a hill to Morgan le Fay's cas-tle, Grandpa," replied Angelica.

"And a good thing, too. We can get out of this rain!" said Grandpa Lou.

The castle was tall, gloomy, and dark gray. Bats darted in and out of the towers and occasionally swooped low near the cart. The moat was black and ominous. Tommy noticed long, shiny black things surfacing and then resubmerging, and hoped Chuckie hadn't noticed them too. Probably alligators, he thought to himself.

As they sat looking at the castle, a loud creaking sound broke the silence, and a shadow fell over them. The drawbridge was being lowered.

"In we go, then!" Grandpa said cheerfully. Tommy wondered if his grandpa could see just how creepy the castle looked. Probably not, without his glasses, Tommy decided.

The cart trundled slowly across the drawbridge. Inside the castle it was dark, damp, and quiet. And then suddenly they heard a loud thunderclap and saw a flash of blue light. When the smoke cleared, there stood a beautiful woman in a long, serpent-green dress. Her skin was white, her lips bloodred, and her hair as black as coal. She smiled at them. "Welcome to my castle," she said sweetly. "I have been expecting you!"

"Tommy," whispered Chuckie, "didn't Addy say Morgan le Fay was a witch?"

"Yes. Twice," said Tommy.

"Where's her black hat and stuff?" asked Chuckie.

Angelica stood up, put her hands on her hips, and faced Morgan le Fay. "How about if you start by tellin' me where my doll is?" she demanded, looking past Morgan into the shadowy hallway.

Morgan laughed musically. "What a delightful child!" she said.

Phil and Lil exchanged uneasy looks. Chuckie tried to hide behind Tommy. Grandpa Lou climbed out of the cart and came over to where Morgan stood. "Howdy do, ma'am?" he asked warmly. "Name's Lou. Lou Pickles, at your service!"

"You must be the great magician I have heard so much about," said Morgan. "I am sure there are many tricks you can teach me." She took Grandpa by the arm and led him out of the hall. To a servant she hissed, "Cage these brats."

The servant grumbled ill-naturedly as he lifted all the babies down from the cart. They heard a trumpet sound from outside the castle. "Not another traveling salesman!" he muttered to himself. "A pox on them! I just dumped boiling oil onto the *last* one. You stay here while I go take care of him!" he said sternly to the babies. He trotted out of the hall and up a curving staircase, leaving Angelica and the babies alone.

"Where do you think Sir Nedd and the other knightses are, Tommy?" asked Chuckie.

"Prob'ly in the dumbgeon. Let's search for them," Tommy replied.

"Here's a door," Angelica said, trotting over to a heavy door that was not much taller than her head. "Let's try down there."

It took all of their strength, but at last the door began to open. They stared at a narrow flight of damp stone stairs, which disappeared into murky darkness.

"Who's first?" Chuckie gulped.

"Sorcerlesses first!" Angelica cried.

Tommy and the other babies exchanged looks and then shrugged. They followed Angelica down the stairs.

The stairs seemed to lead down, down, down forever. When they finally arrived at the bottom, it took a few minutes for their eyes to adjust to the dim light. There seemed to be a room at that end, blocked with bars from floor to ceiling, and they headed toward it.

Angelica was the first to reach the barred room. As the rest of the babies approached, they heard the rattling of chains.

The babies peered into the cell. It was too

dark to see much. The air smelled like damp and rotting things. Inside the room, close to the bars, was a wooden bucket with some muddy-looking water, and next to it, the remains of a moldy loaf of bread.

"Who goes there? Are you friend or foe?" said a deep voice. A face appeared at the bars. It was the face of a man, pale and unshaven. Then another face, and another, and another appeared, all accompanied by the noisy clank-ing of chains.

"Are you the missing knightses from the Camel Lot?" asked Angelica.

"I be Sir Nedd of Nutt," said the first man.

Chuckie gasped. It was Adelaide's father.

"We've come to rescue my doll!" said Angelica. "And you, too," she added. "Is that Sir Casey in there?"

"Yes, I am Sir Casey," another knight said, stepping into the feeble, flickering light.

"Hand over my doll, please," demanded Angelica.

Sir Casey sighed. "The statue that I found in the sand pit, you mean? Alas, Morgan le Fay has taken the doll from me and given it to her sniveling child, Mordred, to play with."

"What?" Angelica said in disbelief.

"You heard him," came a voice behind the babies. They all jumped and turned around. Mordred stood there in the dim corridor, holding Cynthia. She was dressed in rags and was dirty from head to foot.

"Mordred! You give me back my doll!" growled Angelica.

Mordred trotted toward the staircase, with Angelica in pursuit.

Mordred stopped at the foot of the stairs and whirled around, holding Cynthia high above his head. "Stop!" he yelled. "If you come another step, I'll have my mom turn your doll into a pig!"

Angelica stopped in her tracks. "You wouldn't dare!" she said.

"Oh, wouldn't I?" sneered Mordred. "My mom is the meanest witch in the kingdom!"

"Well, you'd better get your mom to let those knightses outta that dumbgeon," said Tommy.

Mordred looked at the grimy doll in his

hand. Then he looked over at the babies. A nasty little smile spread over his face. "I gotta idea," Mordred said with an evil little laugh. "How about we make a little trade?"

"What kind of a trade?" Tommy asked warily.

Mordred pulled a cord that was hanging from the ceiling, which the babies hadn't noticed before. Within seconds a servant appeared. He seemed very much afraid of Mordred. "Yes, Master Mordred, sir?" he said, bowing low to the ground.

"Go fetch Mommy's list of knightly deeds," said Mordred.

The servant disappeared as quickly as he had arrived. A minute later he was back, holding a scroll that was tied with a dark green ribbon.

"That will be all," Mordred said with a wave of his hand. Mordred turned to Tommy, Angelica, Chuckie, Phil, and Lil. "Okay," he said. "You want those knightses free? You want your doll back?"

The babies nodded. Angelica stomped her foot in frustration but, realizing she had no choice, also nodded.

"Okay, then. All you gotta do is go on a quest and perform every one of these knightly deeds. My mom gives this to every knight she finds who's out looking for the Holy Grail."

"What kind of deedses are they, anyway?" asked Tommy.

"Wouldn't you like to know?" he sneered. "The knights think my mom is the only one who knows how to find the Grail, so they all agree to try. She tells the knights that if they can perform every deed on the list, she'll let them have a glimpse of the Grail."

"So your mom knows where to find the Holey Pail?" asked Phil.

"'Course not. No one does. She just says that so she can put the knightses into our dumbgeon. No one has ever been able to accomplish the deeds. The knightses usually fail after the first one."

"I don't care about doing any deedses or see-ing any dumb old pail," said Angelica. "I want my doll!"

"Yeah, and we want the knightses to get free," added Tommy.

"Let me finish," Mordred said irritably. "We'll make a deal: If you can do every one of these deeds, I'll tell my mom she has to free the knightses in our dumbgeon, *and* I'll give the doll back. Got it?"

"Yeah, okay, and what happens if we can't do all of them?" asked Angelica.

"Well, you'll probably not even survive the first deed, so that's a stupid question," he said. "But I promised my mom I would take care of any annoying babies that might get in the way of her ruling Camelot. If I do a good job, she's going to give me my own magic wand."

Chuckie trembled a little bit.

"So," Mordred went on, "supposing you manage to stay alive but can't do all the deeds—well, you gotta come back here and get put in the dumbgeon along with the rest of the knights."

"Why would we be dumb enough to come back here to get put in your dumbgeon?" asked Angelica.

"That's easy," said Mordred. "Because my mom plans to keep your grandpa here until you get back."

54

There was a stunned silence. Mordred looked around at their shocked faces and shrugged. "Don't worry, she won't put him in the dumbgeon or anything. He can stay upstairs as long as he continues to amuse her. She seems to like him, for some reason. But there's no telling how long that will last. Anyway, it's up to you, of course."

Tommy was mad. He took the list out of Mordred's hand. "Okay, we'll go on a quest and do all these knightedly deeds." Tommy looked around at his friends. "The only thing is, none of us can read yet. How do we know what the list says?"

"Don't worry, I gave you the enchanted version," said Mordred. "All you gotta do is touch your finger to the words, and they read themselves to you!" And with that, Mordred clattered up the dungeon steps and was gone.

"I think he's trying to make us go away and never come back," said Lil.

"Well, we gotta go do these deeds," said Tommy. "We got no choice if we're going to rescue my grandpa from Morgan le Fay. Let's get started. But before we leave, I want to make sure my grandpa is all right."

Before they started up the stairs, Angelica trotted back down the corridor, where the knights stood blinking dully at her. "We'll be back soon, guys," she reassured them. "Just as soon as we do some deedses."

Sir Casey spoke. "Then woe is me, for you shall not succeed in these dangerous deeds, child. We shall see you behind these bars anon."

"Don't bet on it!" Angelica said, and turned to trot back down the hallway.

Back upstairs, the babies heard Morgan laugh as they crawled quietly along one side of the hall toward the open doorway to peer through. Grandpa was showing Morgan his brochures. She seemed very interested in them. The remains of a feast were nearby, and Grandpa seemed happy and comfortable.

"Don't worry, Grandpa," Tommy whispered softly. "We'll be back to rescue you."

They crawled the rest of the way out of the great hall. Their cart, with the donkeys and cow, stood just outside, and the drawbridge was down.

"Who's gonna drive the cart now that your grandpa isn't here?" asked Chuckie.

"I am,"Angelica said firmly, clambering into the driver's seat. "That Mordred has met his match. I'm gonna show him he can't get away with kidnapping my doll."

"Or keeping our grandpa shut up in this scary castle," added Tommy.

"Yeah. That too," said Angelica. And off they went.

CHAPTER 6

Tommy unrolled the scroll of paper and peered at the first item on the list. "What was it Mordred said we were supposed to do?" he asked the others.

"He said just point to it, and it'll tell us what to do," said Chuckie.

Tommy pointed at the first line of the list. As he moved his finger along the line, they heard a deep, gravelly voice speak: "The first knightly deed is to rescue four-and-twenty maidens from the Terrible Tower."

They all looked at one another blankly. "Where is the terrible towel?" asked Chuckie.

"How should I know?" snapped Angelica.

"Did that voice come right out of the paper?" asked Lil.

"Yeah, it did," said Tommy. "It kinda sounds

like the sign my dad talks to when he leans outta the car window to buy us doughnuts."

"Do you think *that* could be the Terrible Towel?" Lil asked, pointing at a tower in the distance.

They all looked. The road they were on seemed to head directly to it. The tower was made of stone, with no visible entrance. At the top, a series of windows could be seen running all the way around, and out of the windows they could just make out some lily-white hands holding fluttery white lace handkerchiefs.

"It looks like those ladies are trying to tell us something," said Phil.

"Are they the fourteen-twenny maidens we're supposed to rescue?" Lil wanted to know.

"I can't count that high," admitted Tommy.

"Me either," said Chuckie. "But it does look like a lot of maidens. Whatever a maiden is."

"How are we going to rescue them?" asked Lil. "We can't climb that high even if we stood on each others' shoulders."

"Don't you babies know how to do anything?"

scoffed Angelica. She sprang down from the cart. "Just leave it to the great sorcerless." She stomped toward the tower. At the base of the tower, Angelica put her hands to her mouth and yelled up. "Hey! We heard that you guys need rescuing. Is that true?"

Twenty-four heads poked out of eight windows. Long hair tumbled down, of all different colors. Angelica was suddenly overcome by a powerful blast of perfume, which set her coughing.

"Why, where are the knights in shining armor? You're just a child!" called down one of the maidens. "And the cart over there is full of mere babes!"

"Yeah, so?" Angelica said after she had recovered from her coughing fit. "We've come to rescue you!"

"We four-and-twenty maidens have been imprisoned in this tower for a year and a day!" said the same maiden, who apparently acted as the spokeswoman. "A horrible giant is keeping us prisoners here. We await a fair knight to come to our rescue, but so far no one has been able to defeat the giant. Many have tried, and we know not what became of them. But every day we wait, hoping the next knight will be successful."

"Well, it looks like all the fair knights are tied up at the moment," said Angelica dryly. "So, where is the giant now?"

Twenty-four fingers pointed in the direction of a clump of trees. "He's over there by that stream; every afternoon he takes a three-hour nap. At any moment he shall awake. Be careful that you are not spotted!"

"Spotted?" Tommy said to himself. He had also climbed out of the cart and had come over to stand next to Angelica. "Spotted! Of course! Psssst!" he said to Angelica. Tommy whispered something in her ear.

She nodded. "Not a bad idea for a baby." Then she looked back up at the maidens, who were peering down at her expectantly. "Hey!" she called up to them. "Do you maiden ladies by any chance have any lipstick?"

"Why, of course, child!" called the maiden spokeswoman. "We never know when a knight might appear to rescue us, so we make sure we always look lovely just in case. Shall we throw them down to you?"

"Yeah, fire away!" Angelica said, and immediately she and Tommy were pelted by a rain of lipsticks. "Ow! Okay! Okay! Enough, already!" She scooped up as many as she could. "Don't go anywhere!" she called to the maidens, who, though puzzled, waved their lacy handkerchiefs at her as she and Tommy ran away.

"What are you guys up to, anyway?" Chuckie wanted to know as Tommy and Angelica reached the cart.

"Don't worry, Chuckie," said Tommy. "Angelica and I have everything under control."

"That's what I was afraid of," he murmured.

"Pssssst!" hissed Tommy, nudging Angelica in the ribs. "Look over there!" At first he had thought it was a small hill, but then he noticed that it rose and fell gently, and he realized it must be the giant's stomach.

They crept closer. It was a giant baby, sleeping soundly, wearing a large diaper. He was about as long as a school bus. His blanket, which he held clutched tightly in one hand, was the size of a parachute. Tommy whispered something in Angelica's ear, and together the two of them crept toward the sleeping baby giant's head. Angelica handed something to Tommy.

"What are they doing?" Chuckie whispered to Phil and Lil as he joined them in the bushes.

"It looks like they're drawing something on his face with the lipstick," Lil whispered back.

"Oops. Looks like naptime is over. The giant baby is waking up!" whispered Phil.

Sure enough, the baby giant twitched his giant nose a couple of times, then yawned. Slowly he began to sit up. Tommy and Angelica scampered out of the way of his hand, which was groping around on the ground near them. His hand came to rest upon what it was searching for: a giant baby bottle. The baby picked up the bottle, shoved it into his mouth, took a few sips of milk, then sat up and opened his eyes.

"Look! It has spots all over its face," whispered Lil.

"I think they're lipstick spots," whispered Phil.

Just then the giant noticed Tommy and Angelica, and pulled the bottle out of his mouth with a deafening pop. "Hey!" he thundered. "Aren't you going to run away?"

Tommy stepped bravely toward the giant. He was about one-fourth the size of the giant's bottle. "Uh no, we're not," he called up to the baby, yelling as loud as he could to be heard. "We were just passing by."

"You mean, you're not here to rescue all my real dolls from my tower?" the baby asked with surprise.

"Are those *your* dolls over there?" Tommy shouted.

"Yeah."

"Why do you have them locked up in that tower?" yelled Angelica.

"Because they always try to run away. They're my princess dolls. I like to play with them. But they bite."

"No way are we going to try to rescue them," said Angelica. "Who'd want to play with *them*? I mean, look what happened to you!"

The baby's eyes narrowed. "Whaddaya

64

mean, what happened to me? What *did* happen to me?"

"Well," said Tommy, "you oughtta see yourself! You're obviously allergic to those maidens."

"You have spots all over your face!" added Angelica.

The baby giant looked at them with alarm, and then leaned over to glance at his reflection in a nearby pool of water. He gasped, and a hand flew up to his face.

"If I were you, I wouldn't touch those maidens again," cautioned Tommy.

"But they're in my tower!" wailed the baby giant. "How am I going to get them out of there without touching them? I'll break out in spots all over my body next!"

Tommy pretended to think for a moment. "I got just the thing!" he yelled. "But we'll need to borrow your bottle for a minute."

The baby giant looked horrified, and clutched the bottle tightly to himself. "But it's my ba-ba!" he cried, his lower lip beginning to tremble.

"Don't worry, we'll bring it right back. We

just need some of the milk," Tommy reassured him. "You want to get those maidens outta there, don't you? You don't want to play with something that makes you break out in spots, do you?"

"I guess not," the baby giant said.

"Be right back!" called Tommy. He and Angelica began to roll the huge bottle out of the clearing and toward the Terrible Tower. Chuckie, Phil, and Lil watched them in astonishment.

"Don't just stand there, you three," panted Angelica. "Help us roll this thing!"

At the base of the tower it took all of them several tries to get the top unscrewed, but they finally felt it give and milk gushed out, instantly forming a big, muddy, milky moat.

The maidens were hiding inside. "Hey, maiden ladies!" Angelica called up.

Instantly twenty-four heads peered out of the window, and then twenty-four hands waved to Angelica.

"There's a nice big puddle of milk down here for you to jump into!" she called. "Heave-ho!"

"What?" squeaked the main maiden from above. "And spoil our lovely dresses and muss our lovely curls? You must be joking, child!"

"No, I'm not!" Angelica called back. "Listen here! Do you want to get rescued or don't you? If you do, you'd better hurry or that baby giant is going to change his mind!"

The twenty-four faces disappeared from the window to discuss what to do. A moment later they reappeared. "All right!" the head maiden called in a quavering voice. She shimmied her shoulders and hips out of the window, looked down briefly, closed her eyes, and jumped.

SPLAT!

She landed waist-deep in the milk. She grimaced as the milk splattered on her face. One by one the rest of the maidens jumped until they were all down safely, most of them covered from head to toe in milk.

"Yum," Phil said as he used his hands to slurp up some milk from the moat.

"Yeah, yum," agreed Lil. "Muddy milk!"

Tommy and Angelica rolled the now-empty bottle back over to the giant.

"There you go!" Tommy said to the baby. "I'm sure the spots'll go away in no time!"

"Thanks!" the giant baby called back.

"By the way," Tommy called, "have you seen any knightses recently?"

"Yeah, my mom and dad have them inprisoned in our castle over the mountain," the giant baby said cheerfully. "I think they're going to eat them for lunch today." He picked up his bottle between two huge fingers and turned to wash it in the stream.

Angelica and Tommy hurried back across the glade to where the maidens were cleaning themselves off as best they could. "Okay, maidens, I'd scat if I were you," Angelica said.

"The child has saved us!" exclaimed one dripping maiden. "Are you a sorceress?" she asked.

"Yeah, well, sort of," Angelica said modestly, turning to head back toward the cart.

"Here is a gift from us," the maiden called, trotting after her. She handed Angelica a lacy white handkerchief. Wrapped inside it was a bottle of perfume. "Take this as our thanks."

Angelica looked at the bottle. "This'll keep the mosquitoes away," she muttered to herself. She chucked it into the cart. Then she and the babies watched them all hurry away.

"That deed is done!" Chuckie said happily. "Nice going, you guys! Now can we go back to the Camel Lot?"

"'Fraid not, Chuckie," said Tommy.

"What's the next deed?" asked Lil.

Reluctantly Chuckie unrolled the scroll. He pointed his finger at the second line. The voice spoke: "The second knightly deed is to rescue the knights held captive in the giants' castle."

"That must be the baby giant's mom and dad's house," said Tommy. "He just told me that's where they're keeping all the knightses, and that the giants want to eat the knightses for lunch."

"We're doomed, doomed," moaned Chuckie.

CHAPTER 7

As the cart creaked down the other side of the small mountain, the babies could see the giants' castle looming just ahead. The babies' cart pulled up to the front.

"Well, since we can't get across the moat," said Chuckie, "we might as well give up."

"What? And lose Cynthia forever?" said Angelica.

"And Grandpa?" said Tommy.

"And Addy's daddy?" said Phil and Lil together.

"Okay, okay," said Chuckie. "But how are we going to get in?"

"Look," said Angelica, pointing. A wagon had just rolled up. MEDIEVAL MARKET: FREE DELIVERY was written on the side. One of the deliverymen hopped down and rang the bell of the castle, and the drawbridge began to lower. Angelica was studying the back of the wagon and had a thoughtful look on her face.

"It looks like that wagon is full of groceries," said Phil.

"Are you thinking what I think you're thinking?" Chuckie asked Angelica weakly.

"Great idea, Angelica!" said Tommy. "We'll hide in the groceries and get snuggled in!"

They crawled toward the back of the truck and hoisted themselves up and inside. Tommy hid in a crate full of gigantic loaves of bread. Angelica hid in a crate of vegetables and covered herself with enormous lettuce leaves. Phil hid in a bin full of apples. Chuckie found a bunch of giant bananas, quickly peeled one, and hid inside the empty peel. Lil started to climb into a barrel, then realized it was full of honey. So she jumped into Phil's apple bin just in time.

The deliverymen unloaded the barrels and crates and rolled them across the drawbridge. They deposited them just inside the castle's courtyard, and then Angelica and the babies heard them clatter back over the drawbridge and trot away.

The babies had just enough time to climb

out of their hiding places and hide behind a pillar when the ground began to tremble. They heard footsteps, which grew louder and louder until they were nearly deafening. As Angelica and the babies watched from their hiding places, two enormous giants appeared. They were easily twice the size of the baby giant.

The male giant sniffed the air. "Fee Fie Fo Fum! I smell some peppermint chewing gum!"

Angelica, who had just popped the gum into her mouth a few moments before, stopped chewing and then swallowed hard.

"Nah," said the female giant. "You're just hungry. You smell the mint I ordered for your tea. Come on, help me carry these groceries into the kitchen. Then I will boil up the knights and serve them to you for lunch with a bit of applesauce and vegetable stew, just the way you like them!"

The male giant grumbled a bit, but picked up one of the barrels and carried it away. The female giant picked up another and followed after her husband.

"Don't tell me. Let me guess," whispered

Chuckie. "We're going to follow those gigantics into the kitchen."

"Yes, Chuckie," Tommy whispered back.

Tommy led the way, crawling ever so quietly toward the kitchen. The rest of the babies followed him. As they peered around the doorjamb, they could just make out an enormous birdcage sitting on the counter. It was covered with a cloth, but they could hear voices from within.

"Our time is running out, Sir Dean," came one voice from inside the cage. "The groceries hath just been delivered, and with them our certain demise approacheth."

"Aye, Sir Cumference, 'tis true. The giants mean to eat us for their lunch."

"If only we could escape from this cage. We could do battle with the giants," said a third voice.

"I fear we have no way out of our cage, Sir Askinfort," the second voice said sadly.

Tommy turned to the rest of the babies and Angelica. "The knightses are locked up in that cage," he whispered. "The gigantics are going to eat them for lunch."

"I got it! Let's run for it!" suggested Chuckie.

"We gotta think of a way to get up to that counter," said Tommy. The countertop was as high as the ceiling in his bedroom.

"We could open those drawers and climb up that way," suggested Lil.

Angelica looked at the drawers. Then she looked at Lil. "I can't believe I didn't think of that!" she said.

"Come on, you guys," whispered Tommy. "We have to hurry!"

Angelica boosted everyone into the bottom drawer. "Ow, Chuckie, you just stepped on my head!" she snapped.

"Sorry, Angelica," Chuckie whispered back. Angelica then ran back to their hiding place to watch as the four babies opened the next drawer.

Chuckie boosted the other three into it. Then he, too, climbed back down and joined Angelica in hiding.

Next, Tommy boosted Phil and Lil. Giving them an encouraging thumbs-up sign, he, too, climbed back down.

Phil helped his sister up to the counter. He, too, climbed down to watch with the others.

Lil inched her way along the counter toward the cage. The knights were silent. She passed a dog's leash and a huge pepper grinder, and was nearly at the cage when the female giant came stomping across the kitchen.

"How did those drawers get open, I wonder?" she thundered, and slammed them all closed.

"Oh, no!" said Phil. "How is Lil gonna get back down now?"

The others could only watch in silent horror as the giant marched over to the cage and took off the cover. There sat three miserable knights, their mustaches drooping dejectedly.

"Lil got the cage door open!" said Tommy excitedly. Sure enough, Lil had managed to duck underneath the cover of the cage and slide out the latch pin before the giant pulled the cover off the cage.

The giant started to reach toward the cage door, but her hand stopped. "Blast," she rumbled. "I almost forgot to salt the stew." She stepped away from the cage and walked over toward the stove, rummaging noisily among the jars and bottles just next to it.

"Now what's Lil doing?" whispered Chuckie. "Tell me what happens. I can't look."

"She's got the dog leash," said Tommy. "And she's swinging it over her head like a lasso. She just looped it around the pepper grinder. And now she's dumped the other end of the leash off the counter. Good idea, Lil!"

"She's climbing down!" said Phil.

Meanwhile the knights had noticed the unlatched door. "'Tis a miracle, Sir Dean! The door stands open!" said Sir Cumference.

"Let us make haste!" cried Sir Dean. "After you, Askinfort!"

"No, no, I couldn't think of it!" said Askinfort gallantly. "You first, Sir Cumference!"

Suddenly the giant approached the cage again. Throwing chivalry to the winds, all three knights tumbled through the cage door and headed toward the edge of the counter. Lil was practically to the floor. She jumped the rest of the way and ran to join the others.

"Do my eyes play tricks on me?" cried Sir Dean, pointing to the leash that was still looped around the pepper grinder. He began climbing down, followed by the others.

"Look over there," Tommy said, pointing. Across the kitchen they could see a trapdoor in the bottom of the kitchen door. "That looks like Spike's doggie door in our house!"

The words were hardly out of his mouth when the door flapped open and in tumbled a giant dog. The dog bounded up to the giant, causing her to stop and turn toward him. The massive creature slobbered all over her hands.

"There, there, Fang," she said, stooping down to pet him. "Just as soon as I get the vile little creatures into the stew pot, I'll take you for a nice walk, my puddums."

Angelica had darted out toward the knights just as they were dropping to the floor. "Over there, you guys!" she called quietly. "Head for the doggie door!" She pointed toward the door at the end of the kitchen.

"Thank you, child," Sir Dean whispered, and he and his comrades all bowed low. Then they began to work their way across the kitchen.

"See ya back at the Camel Lot!" Angelica called after them. The dog's ears pricked up. He looked around, then gave a bark. Then he began baying so loud, the dishes rattled on the shelves.

"What is it, Fang?" asked the female giant.

"They're doomed!" cried Chuckie. "The dog is gonna get 'em!"

"Wait!" said Lil. "I gotta 'nother idea!"

"You do?" said Angelica.

"Yeah! Help me pull the plug on that barrel right there!" she whispered.

"THEY'RE ESCAPING!" bellowed the female giant. She had spotted the knights, who were now nearly at the doggie door. The male giant came charging into the kitchen.

As the giants trundled clumsily after the knights, who dodged and weaved between their feet, Angelica, Chuckie, Tommy, Phil, and Lil pulled at the cork at the bottom of the barrel with all their might. For a moment they thought it wouldn't budge. But finally it popped out, causing all the babies to land on top of each other in a heap.

Honey flowed out in a thick, sticky pool. It streamed across the kitchen floor just as the last knight had thrown himself through the doggie door to freedom. The female giant was the first to step into it. Her foot caught, sending her tumbling downward to the floor like a falling tree. Next the male giant got stuck and fell, the tremor at impact rattling every dish on the shelves. Finally, the honey reached Fang's back leg. He whirled around to try to bite it free, and tumbled right over into the pool of stickiness, causing him to howl with anger. None of them could budge. The noise was deafening.

"Let's get outta here!" called Angelica. She and the babies scurried around the pool of honey and out the doggie door.

The drawbridge was still down, and their cart was still there. They all climbed in, and Angelica shook the reins.

"Look!" said Lil. "There are the knightses!"

"Thanks to you again!" called the knights, who were heading toward Camelot as fast as their chain mail would let them. "Until we meet again!"

The cart creaked away from the giants' castle.

"Good job, Lillian!"

"We did it, Philip!"

"Let's get outta here!" yelled Chuckie.

CHAPTER 8

Chuckie took out the list. "Two deeds done," he said with a smile. He was starting to enjoy rescuing knights.

As the cart creaked over hill and dale, the day grew warmer and warmer, and the road got dustier and dustier.

"I'm hot!" Angelica complained.

"Back at the Camel Lot, we could be swimming in our fancy pool right now," Lil said wistfully.

"Well, why don't we stop and take a swim?" Tommy suggested. "There's a little stream in that meadow right there."

"It looks like there used to be a big pond over there," said Chuckie. "See? There's a huge, muddy hole. I wonder where all the water went."

"Who cares?" said Angelica, reining the

donkeys and leaping out of the cart. "The stream is good enough for me right now."

"Come on, Lil, let's go make mud pies!" Phil said.

"Okay. Maybe we'll find a few worms!"

While the other three splashed about happily in the little stream, the twins toddled over to the muddy banks and began happily squishing around in the mud.

"Hey, look at this," Phil said, holding something up for Lil to see.

"What do you think it is?" Lil asked, sliding over to her brother's side to check it out.

It was a small rubber-like disk, attached to a metal chain that was still stuck in the ground. Angelica and Tommy jumped out of the water and came over to have a look.

"That looks like the stopper thing from my bathtub," said Tommy.

"Maybe it's s'posed to plug up a drain somewhere?" suggested Lil.

Angelica shrugged and looked away. "No drains around here," she said. "Hey! A plum tree!" Angelica handed the rubber thing back to

Phil and ran over to the tree to pick some plums. Tommy and Chuckie joined her, and the three began collecting the ripe fruit from the low-hanging branches.

"What are you going to do with it?" Lil asked her brother.

Phil shrugged. "Nothing, I guess," he said. "Let's go swimming." As Lil went to jump into the stream, Phil tossed the rubber stopper onto the muddy bank. Then he joined his sister.

Meanwhile the rubber stopper rolled back down the embankment, coming to rest in a little drain hole that no one had noticed. The level of the water started to rise. The muddy place was becoming a small pool.

Back under the plum tree, Tommy turned to Chuckie. "So, what's the next deed, Chuckie?" he asked.

Chuckie unscrolled the document and touched at the third deed. The voice spoke: "The third knightly deed is to restore water to the Well of Wellington."

There was silence all around. "Wella-Wellington?" Chuckie said finally.

Tommy pointed at a small town in the distance. "Maybe the people who live there will know," he said.

"Hey, does the water look like it's getting higher?" Chuckie asked, pointing at the stream. It was now a small lake.

"Maybe a little," said Tommy.

"Yeah, well, whatever. Who cares about the water. Let's get going and finish the deeds," said Angelica.

Everyone hopped back onto the cart, and they headed toward the town.

As they rolled through the gates of the town, villagers lined the streets, watching the cart pass. Many people bowed down low; others cheered.

"They sure look like they've been suspecting me," Angelica said, smoothing her hair and patting her dress.

As the cart reached the center of town, it was quickly surrounded by villagers. Angelica was lifted down and escorted to a seat of honor in a cushiony chair. The babies were set down on soft pillows nearby.

A man who appeared to be the mayor knelt down low before Angelica. "We welcome you, Lady Angelica, the great and powerful sorceress. We have heard much of your talent, and wish you Godspeed in restoring the well."

"Uh, how did you hear about me?" Angelica asked, a little flustered.

"You are famous throughout Arthur's realm. You have freed the four-and-twenty maidens from the Terrible Tower, and the knights from the giants' castle. Word travels quickly around the kingdom."

"Oh. Ah," said Angelica, shifting uncomfortably. "Okay, so now you need us, I mean, you need me to do something around here for you, is that it? So, what's up?"

"It is our well. It has run dry." He pointed sadly at a stone structure in the center of the town's square. "For thousands of years it flowed, supplying our town with its source of water. But then one day the lake over there began to shrink." He pointed toward the meadow outside of town, near where the babies had gone for a swim. "No one knows why. Most believe some angry magician has cast a spell and caused it to run dry. We are in big trouble. Our stores have nearly dried up. We cannot live without the water."

"'Tis dirty work afoot!" shouted one of the villagers from the crowd.

"'Tis the doing of Morgan le Fay!" shouted someone else. "She caused the water to run dry!"

The mayor continued sadly. "So you see, O Great Sorceress, that we have been waiting for you. Now, go ahead, please, and do your magic stuff."

Angelica's eyes narrowed. "What's in it for me if I fix it?" she asked.

"Angelica!" Tommy gasped, horrified. "Isn't doing the deed good enough?"

"Shush," Angelica hissed back at him.

The mayor clasped his hands together in a pleading gesture. "Our everlasting gratitude," he said.

"Uh-huh," said Angelica.

"And all the pies you can eat."

"Now you're talking," said Angelica. "Okay,

uh, I'm going to need some room, please, in order to perform this mirable. If everyone could step back . . . that's right, but even more, please. More. THANKS!" she shouted as the villagers retreated to the farthest corners of the square.

"What do we do now?" she hissed at the others.

"Well, we'd better think of something fast," Tommy said.

"But what, Tommy?" said Chuckie. "We're just babies. We can't make the water come back."

"I know," Tommy agreed. "At home my mom just calls the plumber when the water doesn't work."

"What does a plumber do?" asked Chuckie.

"I don't really know," said Tommy.

"Hey!" said Phil. "Maybe plumbers fix stuff with plums! Why don't we try it? We could try dropping some plums down the well and see what happens!"

"It just might work," said Tommy.

"Yeah, well, let's give it a whirl," said Angelica. She hopped up and ran over to the cart. She rummaged around until she came up with several plums from the basket. Then she hurried over to the well and dropped them down one at a time. After a couple of seconds, they all heard a faint *plop*, and then another and another.

"So, what do we do now?" asked Chuckie.

"I guess we wait for the plums to do their stuff," said Tommy.

Suddenly they heard a gurgling sound. The townspeople, who were still standing at a respectful distance from the babies in the far corners of the square, had heard it too. There was a shout, and then a roar. Several of them ran over to the well and peered down. Others pointed through the gap in the buildings, toward the place outside of town where the babies had recently been swimming. Where the stream had been was now a large, sparkling lake.

The mayor raced over and clasped Angelica's hand. "The child has performed a wondrous miracle! The water of the Well of Wellington has been restored!"

A cheer rose up. Angelica found herself

hoisted high into the air. She waved and smiled. Maybe the plums had worked after all? Villagers began running up to the cart and heaping it high with steaming pies. "Thank you! Thank you!" called Angelica, bowing graciously to the villagers. "Uh, guess we'll be going along now!"

After they were back in their cart, the grateful shouts of the villagers still rang in their ears. They headed through the gates of the town and back onto the road again.

"I guess the plums fixed it," said Tommy. "Good thinkin', Phil."

"Yeah, well, remember who spotted them first," Angelica said, coolly polishing her knuckles and lying back to relax.

Phil and Lil looked at each other and rolled their eyes.

"Three deeds done!" Chuckie beamed.

CHAPTER 9

The cart creaked up a hill and down the other side. As it approached a bridge, Chuckie pulled out the scroll and touched his finger to it.

The voice spoke: "The fourth knightly deed is to answer the riddles of the Babe of the Bridge."

"Huh?" said Chuckie. "I wonder what that's supposed to mean. What babe—"

"HALT!" boomed a loud voice from below.

"Who was that?" Chuckie asked, clutching Tommy's shirt.

"Who's there?" Tommy called.

Suddenly something sprang in front of the cart, causing the two donkeys to stop short and the cow to bump into Angelica from behind.

"Hey!" Angelica said, rubbing her shoulder. "What's the big idea, jumpin' in front of us like that? Who do you think you are?"

"I am the Babe of the Bridge!" said the baby, who didn't look much bigger than Tommy.

"You are?" said Tommy. "Well, that's lucky, because you're our next deed. And you don't even look scary."

"Well, I am," he replied, trying to lower his voice a little and furrow his brow. "And none of the knightses before you were able to answer my riddles, so I'd be really scareded if I were you."

"Okay," Tommy said, climbing down from the cart. "I guess it's my turn. What do I gotta do?"

"You gotta answer my three riddles," said the baby. "If you guess them, you can cross the bridge."

"What happens if I get them wrong?" asked Tommy.

"You get sent to Morgan's le Fay's dumbgeon. That's what happened to all the knightses. None of them could guess the answers to my riddles."

"Tommy, let's just forget the whole thing and call it a day," Chuckie called from the cart.

Tommy turned to look at his friend. "I can't do that, Chuckie," he said. "I gotta save my grandpa!" He turned back to the Babe of the Bridge. "Okay. What's my first riddle?"

The Babe of the Bridge cleared his throat and looked Tommy right in the eye. Then he spoke very slowly:

"Think on this hard; be sure that you're right.
What is important to have for the night?"

Tommy didn't hesitate. "A blankie, of course."

The baby took a stunned step backward. "That's correct. Good job."

Chuckie let out a whoop from the cart.

"Thanks," said Tommy.

"Practically all of the knightses got that one wrong. They all thought I was asking what is important to have for the *knight*. Most of them said stuff like, 'The knight needs his horse and his trusty sword,' but a *blankie* is what you need at night." The baby eyed Tommy with new respect. "Ready for the next one?"

"Yep."

The baby cleared his throat:

"Here's the next riddle, a much harder test.
When is a change a change for the best?"

Tommy looked at the Babe of the Bridge. He blinked once, twice, and then replied: "When you gots a dirty diaper?"

"Right!"

Phil and Lil did a double high five and a chest bump.

The Babe of the Bridge shook his head in disgust. "You'd be amazed how many of the knightses got that wrong. They thought I meant a change of seasons and stuff. They said things like, 'When winter changes to spring, and spring changes into summer . . .' But you got the right answer."

The Babe of the Bridge crossed his arms and fixed his gaze on Tommy. "Ready for the third riddle?"

"Go ahead."

"Here goes." The baby cleared his throat dramatically. "Fill in the blank: It is the rash fool who goes to battle without . . ."

Tommy looked at the Babe of the Bridge carefully. "Dipey-rash cream?"

Phil, Lil, Chuckie, and Angelica held their collective breath.

The Babe of the Bridge looked at Tommy. "Yessirree."

Everyone in the cart let out a cheer.

Tommy breathed a sigh of relief.

"The knightses all said 'sword' or 'trusty steed.' I thought that was the easiest of all," the Babe of the Bridge said, shaking his head.

"Well, no offense or anything," said Tommy, "but none of the riddles seemed too hard."

The baby nodded. "Yeah, I know. But you'd be surprised how many of the knightses couldn't guess them. You guys want to stay and have lunch with me before you go over the bridge? I'm havin' strained peaches and cream."

"No thanks," said Tommy. "We've got some more deedses to do." He climbed back into the cart.

"How many deeds do you have left?" called the baby.

Chuckie pulled out the list and counted the lines.

"Two," Chuckie replied.

"Here, I got a present for you," said the Babe of the Bridge. He rummaged around in his diaper and pulled out a large golden key. Then he held it out to Tommy. "This key opens any locked door. It's magic. Alls you have to do is point it at the door. Maybe it'll come in handy."

Tommy thanked the baby, and the cart began moving.

"Good luck!" called the Babe of the Bridge as they rolled away.

CHAPTER 10

Chuckie sighed. "I'm the only one of us who hasn't performed a knightly deed," he said sadly. "The problem is, though, that I'm too a-scared to do them!"

"Don't worry, Chuckie," soothed Tommy. "If it'll make you feel better, why don't you try the next one? What does the list say?"

Chuckie touched the list with his finger, and they all heard the voice speak. "The fifth knightly deed is to rescue the princess from a fire-breathing dragon."

"Oh," Chuckie said with relief. "No problem. I should be able to handle that. I thought it was going to be something really scary, like . . . AHHHHH! Did that just say 'a fire-breathing dragon'?"

"I'm afraid so, Chuckie," said Tommy. "But

listen. Angelica and I are the ones with the grandpa who's a prisoner in Morgan's castle, and it's Angelica's doll that's missing, so it's fine if you want Angelica to do this one instead."

"Hey!" Angelica said indignantly. "I did the fourteen-twenny maidens!"

"Well, Angelica, you keep telling everyone that you're such a powerful sorcerless and that you've been doing all this by yourself," said Lil.

"Yeah," said Phil, "so maybe *you* should go fight the dragon!"

"Hold on," said Chuckie. "I promised Addy I would help find her daddy and rescue him if he needed rescuing. And if the only way to do it is to fight a big, scary—" his voice cracked, but he collected himself—"a big, scary fire-breathing dragon, then I guess, um, I guess that's fine! Show me the dragon!"

"Thataway, Chuckie!" Tommy said encouragingly.

"Uh, actually, I think it would be over *that-away*," Angelica said, pointing toward a rocky cave a few hundred yards off the road. They all watched a puff of green smoke rise up into the blue sky. It drifted away on the light breeze.

Chuckie cleared his throat. "Okay, let's go," he said grimly.

As the cart approached the cave, they could hear nothing but silence from within. Angelica pulled up just outside.

Tommy tapped his friend's shoulder. "Chuckie, are you sure about this?" he whispered.

"Yes, Tommy." He pulled out the portrait that Addy had given to him." I keep seein' Addy's face, and remembering when she told us about her daddy, and I know I gotta help her. And your grandpa needs help, Tommy, and you're my bestest friend," he said, his voice breaking slightly. "But just in case I don't come outta there, Tommy . . . tell my daddy I . . . love him. When you get older, of course."

"Okay, Chuckie. Good luck."

Chuckie crept quietly down from the cart and tiptoed up to the mouth of the cave. Suddenly a blast of black smoke poured out, accompanied by a loud roar and then a shriek. Chuckie clutched at the stone entryway, his knees buckling under him a bit.

It took a couple of minutes for the smoke to clear out enough for him to be able to peek inside. Seeing nothing, he stepped cautiously into the cave. He blinked in the semidarkness, then took off his glasses and polished them up. When he'd put them back on, he was not prepared for what met his gaze. Two eyes stared back at him amid the billows of black smoke.

"AHHHHHH!" shrieked Chuckie.

"AHHHHHH!" shrieked a high-pitched voice. And then the owner of the eyes stepped into the dim light. It was a little girl about Chuckie's age. She wore a long purple dress, which was badly soiled. There was a gold crown perched crookedly on top of her brown curly hair. Her face was smudged with soot, but she was grinning at Chuckie. "Hi," she said. "I'm Princess Dinah."

"H-H-Hi," said Chuckie. "I'm Chuckie Finster. Uh, did the dragon just try to light you on fire or somethin'?"

"The dragon?" she scoffed. "Nah, there aren't any dragons around here. I was just doing an esperiment with my chemistry set. My mom won't let me do esperiments in the castle because they make such a mess, so I do them out here in this cave. I'm trying to turn metal into gold, but between you and me, I don't think it's possible. Come on, I'll show ya." She took Chuckie by the hand and pulled him deeper into the cave.

"B-B-But I'm here to rescue you from the fire-breathing dragon," Chuckie said as he trudged along beside her through the narrow passageway. "You are a princess, aren't you?"

"Sure, I'm a princess. My dad is a distant cousin of King Arthur's brother-in-law. We have a little castle over the next hill. But like I said, there aren't any dragons around here. Sorry."

They had just entered a large chamber of the cave. The roof opened high over their heads. Dinah's chemistry experiments lined one wall. Chuckie sat down heavily on a near-by rock. "But if I don't rescue you, then we can't finish the deeds," he said. He buried his face in his hands. "I'm a failure," he moaned.

Dinah sat down next to him and patted his

back. "Gee," she said, "I'm really sorry, but . . ."

Suddenly a large section of the far wall moved to one side, and a low roar filled the cave. Two evil yellow eyes squinted at them from the darkness beyond, and then something appeared in the dim light. A green, scaly creature about the size of Tommy's dog stood before them, arching its long neck and slithering its forked tongue at them. Two puffs of black smoke billowed out of its flared nostrils.

"Wow!" Dinah said, staring at the creature. "I guess that would be a dragon! Well, that's handy, huh? I guess you'd better rescue me now."

Chuckie stood up on shaking knees and faced the creature. The creature took a step toward Chuckie. "Okay, dragon!" he squeaked. "You'd better go back where you came from!"

The dragon blinked its yellow eyes at Chuckie. Then it opened its mouth. A stream of orange flame surged out.

"Watch out, Dinah!" Chuckie yelled, grabbing her by the arm. The two rolled out of the way of the flames just in time. The chamber reeked of smoke.

"If I could only reach my chemistry set, I could find something to throw at it!" said Dinah.

Suddenly Chuckie had an idea. He rummaged around in his pocket. "Stand back, Dinah!" he cried. He took another step toward the creature. "Hey, ya big meanie!" he shouted at it. "Let me see you just try to do that again!"

The dragon blinked at Chuckie again. Then it opened its jaws and took a deep breath, as though preparing to send out an especially strong flame. But just as it tried to, Chuckie pointed something at its open jaws. It was Addy's squirt gun. "Take that!" Chuckie yelled, and he squirted the water into the dragon's jaws.

It worked. The flames were quenched before they had traveled out of the dragon's mouth. Two tiny plumes of black smoke drifted out of its mouth and then vanished. The creature clamped its mouth closed, turned quickly around, and crawled out the way it had come, whimpering the whole time. The rock slid back in front of the opening.

Chuckie stood, breathing hard, holding the empty squirt gun at his side.

"Wow! Nice going, Chuckie!" Dinah said, leaping up and clapping him on the back. "You did it! You rescued me!"

"I did?" Chuckie said, managing a tiny grin.

Dinah linked her arm through Chuckie's and began escorting him toward the opening of the cave. His legs felt like they were made of rubber. "You did a great job, Chuckie," she said. "I have no idea where that dragon came from, but I doubt he'll be back. Here," she said, handing him a tiny cloth purse cinched with a string. "Take some of my alchemy powder from my esperiment as a thank-you present. It doesn't really work, but it's a pretty color."

"Thanks Dinah," Chuckie said happily. "I was pretty brave, wasn't I?"

"Yep. You sure were." She grinned. "Good luck with the rest of your quest."

Chuckie emerged from the cave and blinked in the bright sunlight.

Tommy clambered over the side of the cart and hurried over to his friend. "Chuckie!" he beamed. "You're okay! We thought we'd never see you again!"

Chuckie grinned. Then he walked over and pulled out the scroll. "The fifth knightly deed is all done," he said modestly, checking it off the list. He could feel the others staring at him in astonishment. "Hey, a baby's gotta do what a baby's gotta do." He shrugged.

And off they went.

CHAPTER 11

Chuckie ran his finger down the list of knightly deeds until he reached the last one.

The voice spoke. "The final knightly deed is to joust with the Green Knight and thereby win the hand of the fair maiden."

Chuckie looked up from the scroll and blinked a couple of times. "We may as well turn around right now and go on back to the Camel Lot. I mean, we know what a maiden is now, but does anyone know what 'joust' means?"

"I wonder what maiden they're talking about?" asked Tommy. "And I wonder how she losted her hand and how we're s'posed to win it?"

Angelica sighed impatiently. "Don't you babies know anything? Don't you ever watch the Fairy Tale Channel on cable? To joust means to fight somebody. To win a maiden's hand means to marry her! We gotta fight a knight and knock him off his horse and then we gotta marry a maiden!"

"Don't you gotta be out of diapers before you can marry someone?" asked Phil.

"Good point, Phil," Tommy agreed. "Chuckie and Angelica are the only ones who don't wear diapers anymore."

"Well, I'm still really tired from performing the fifth knightly deed," Chuckie said quickly. "I don't think I can go knock anyone off a horse right now. Or get married," he added.

"Oh, brother. Do I have to do everything around here?" seethed Angelica. "Fine. I'll handle this one." They rode in silence for a few minutes, and then she spoke again. "If it's not too much trouble, maybe you babies could help me find the Green Knight."

With a trembling finger, Chuckie pointed across a lake next to a misty green field. Just past it stood a stone, stadium-like structure. There were no spectators in the stands, which made it seem all the more eerie. Bright flags flapped in the breeze, and they could just make out a figure on a white horse, trotting back and forth across the playing field. The knight steadied a long, evil-looking lance, which was set vertically into a holster on the side of his horse. The horse tossed its head and reared up, but the rider skillfully kept his seat.

"Well, talk about not fair!" fumed Angelica. "How can I work under these conditions! I don't have a horse, or a suit of armchair. If I ever get outta this in one piece, I'll have a thing or two to say to that Morgan about how she doesn't play by the rules."

As they came around the lake and nearer to the stadium, they could see the horseman more clearly. He wore a suit of armor from head to foot, the visor down. A green tunic was draped over his broad shoulders and belted by his sword belt. Three plumed green feathers sprouted from the tip of his helmet. He wore ugly spurs on his feet. His horse, also draped in green, snorted and pawed at the ground and strained at the bit.

"Maybe you could ride on one of our donkeys, Angelica," Lil suggested helpfully.

"Great," Angelica said sarcastically as she hopped down from the cart and began unharnessing one of the donkeys.

"Angelica, he's so big and scary looking!" whispered Chuckie.

Angelica shrugged. "Do you babies have any suggestings as to what I can use for a weapon in this joust?" she said.

Chuckie, Tommy, Phil, and Lil scrambled around, looking in the cart. "Here's a plum," said Phil.

"Here's a lacy white handkerchief with a lot of perfume all over it," said Lil.

"Here's some of Dinah's powder from her chemistry esperiment," said Chuckie.

"Gee, thanks," Angelica said dryly, shoving the items into her pockets. She gave the donkey a pat on the behind, and the babies watched her clop into the field to face the Green Knight.

Neither spoke. The Green Knight merely turned his horse and paced to one end of the field as Angelica and her donkey paced to the other.

"I can't watch this," said Chuckie. "Tell me what happens, Tommy."

When they were both standing and facing one another, the knight suddenly began galloping toward Angelica. As he galloped, he lifted up his deadly lance and began to lower it so that it was aimed directly at her. With his other hand he swung a great sword above his head.

"Uh-oh," said Angelica. Her donkey didn't budge.

Now all the babies hid their eyes.

Just as the knight was about to reach Angelica, her donkey sat down, leaving her well out of reach of the sword and lance. The knight thundered past her. As he pulled up to swing back around, the babies saw something white fluttering from the tip of the lance. "It's the hankie!" Lil squealed in delight. "The Green Meanie got it stuck on his spear!"

"He looks mad," Phil said gleefully.

"Yeah, and not just that," Tommy said, "but I think all the perfume on it is making his horse sneeze!" Sure enough, the horse flared its nostrils and sneezed several times.

Next, Angelica threw the plum at the knight as hard as she could. It bounced along the ground and came to rest just where the stallion was standing. The horse reared up on its hind legs to sneeze again, and came down right on the plum, causing the animal to stumble and then to rear up again.

The knight was now having trouble keeping his balance. Seeing her opportunity, Angelica gave her donkey a pat on its backside and clopped over to where the knight was struggling to remain in his saddle. She pulled out Dinah's pouch and threw some of the purple powder onto the knight.

"Take that!" she said. "Not that I have any clue what this stuff is," she added to herself. The wind picked up the powder and blew it around the knight and his horse in a purple swirl.

The first thing that toppled to the ground at Angelica's feet was the sword. But it looked different. No longer a cold, deadly gray, it now glinted golden in the sunlight. Angelica and the babies barely had time to register this fact before the lance clattered to the ground, followed quickly by the knight himself, who tumbled out of his saddle and landed with a dull thud at Angelica's feet. His armor was now a golden yellow, just like his sword and his lance.

"Hey!" said Angelica. "His suit of armchair turned into gold! Hah! Take that! *Now* are you ready to suspender, you big bully?"

The knight groaned inside his visor.

"So Dinah's esperiment *did* work!" Chuckie said to himself with a smile. "She knows how to change metal into gold!" He and the other babies hurried across the field to where Angelica stood, one foot propped on the chest of the defeated knight.

Tommy stepped up to the knight's helmet and flipped up the visor. They all stared.

"MORDRED!" shrieked Angelica. "Why, why . . . you!" For once, Angelica was speechless.

Mordred glared up at her. "Would you care to refrain from stammering and please step off me? I will need help getting out of this armor," he complained.

"Hold on just a minute," said Tommy. "First,

tell us how you got this Green Knight suit of armchair to turn golden!"

"I don't know why it turned to gold," Mordred said, then turned his head sullenly toward Angelica. "She witched it, I guess. All I know is it suddenly got so heavy, I couldn't stay on my horse. And right now I can't move a muscle, so I would appreciate it if you could unbuckle me and help me outta this."

"But how come you're dressed up like a Green Knight?" Tommy demanded to know.

"Well, I was worried that you guys had accomplished all the rest of the knightly deeds, and I'd promised my mom I'd get rid of you. I started following you a long time ago, to make sure you were permanently out of the picture. But you guys kept accomplishing the deeds. So I decided I would need to fight Angelica myself. I took this horse from one of the knightses in our dumbgeon and followed you guys." He tried to shrug, but the heavy armor prevented it.

"So where's the maiden?" said Phil. "Doesn't Angelica have to marry a maiden?"

Mordred suddenly got a devilish look on his

111

face. "Oh, yeah. Angelica wins the hand of the maiden, doesn't she? Well, unbuckle me from this stuff, and I'll get her for you."

There didn't seem to be much else they could do. Angelica and the babies unbuckled Mordred from his armor, which took quite some time, as it was fastened together in many separate pieces and none of them had learned how to unbuckle yet. When they finally had it all disassembled, Mordred sprang up.

"Okay!" he said. "You get the maiden's hand. Here it is!" And he pulled something from behind his back and thrust it into Angelica's face.

"Cynthia!" she shrieked.

It was Cynthia's hand. Angelica grabbed it out of Mordred's grasp and stared at it in horror.

Mordred gave an evil cackle. "Okay, so you guys accomplished all the deeds. Congratulations. But I never said I'd give you back the whole doll!"

"Mordred, you haven't kepted any of your promises!" said Tommy.

"Hey, all's fair when you're evil," Mordred said, smirking. He looked up at the sky, which was darkening with ominous clouds, then shouted, "MOMMYYYYY!"

Before they knew what had happened, Mordred had vanished in a plume of orange smoke. All that remained were the weapons and pieces of golden armor strewn around the field, as well as his horse, which grazed tranquilly nearby. Angelica shook her fist at the place where Mordred had been standing. "I'll get you back for this, Mordred!" she yelled at the now empty air.

"Now what?" said Lil.

"Yeah, now what?" said Phil.

"I'm trying to 'member what was going to happen once we performed all the knightly deeds," said Tommy. "Mordred said that knightses who did all the deeds expected to get a glimpse of the Holey Pail."

Suddenly the dark clouds parted, and a golden ray of sun shone down directly onto their heads, like a spotlight. It bathed them all in a heavenly glow. The birds ceased their singing, and a group of voices began to sing in unearthly, high-pitched tones. And then a vision materialized in the sky.

"What is it?" whispered Chuckie.

"It looks like a pail," said Angelica.

"A holey pail," said Lil.

"The Holey Pail!" Tommy exclaimed.

The pail spoke. Its voice was deep and resonant, and each of them felt it reverberate through their body. "Pick up the golden sword and carry it away with you," it said. "Then, go to Morgan le Fay's castle and rescue the prisoners. Then, proceed back to Camelot and present the sword to the king."

The singing grew louder until it swelled to one final high note, and then the pail disappeared. The clouds zoomed away. The sky cleared, the sun shone, and the birds resumed their song.

"Wow. I've never seen my holey pail at home do anything like that," said Tommy.

"Let's go, you guys," Angelica said impatiently, picking up the donkey's harness and pulling it toward the cart. "We still have work to do. I gotta get back the rest of Cynthia from that evil Mordred."

"Wait!" Chuckie called. "Aren't we supposed to take the sword back with us?" He pointed at the sword that lay next to all the bits and pieces of armor.

"You're right, Chuckie. That's what the Holey Pail said," Tommy agreed, stooping to pick it up. "This sword sure is heavy. I wonder why King Arthur would want it."

Tommy began dragging the sword toward the cart. Chuckie helped him. The others followed them back to the cart, where Angelica already had the second donkey back in its harness. Together the babies heaved the sword into the back of the cart.

"Wait!" said Tommy. "Mordred said he took that horse from one of the knightses. Maybe we should bring that back to the Camel Lot, too."

The others watched Tommy toddle back out to the field where the magnificent horse stood. It looked down at Tommy for a moment. Then it knelt down so that its forelegs were tucked completely under its body. They watched Tommy climb onto the horse's back, and then the horse stood up slowly and gently with

115

Tommy on its back. Horse and baby trotted over to the cart.

"Gee, Tommy, I didn't know you could ride a horse," said Chuckie.

"It's just like riding my hobbyhorse at home," Tommy said as he turned the horse around to lead the way. "Let's go, you guys!" he said, a new determination in his voice.

"To Morgan's castle!" cried Angelica, giving the reins a shake. And off they all went.

CHAPTER 12

Night fell, and everyone slept soundly while the donkeys plodded back toward Morgan le Fay's castle. Tommy leaned down so that he was resting on the horse's neck, snuggled into its silky mane, and fell asleep.

The next morning Tommy awoke just in time to see the sun rising over the horizon. And in the distance he could see the now-familiar castle of Morgan le Fay. "Wake up, you guys!" said Tommy. "There it is!"

Chuckie opened his eyes and sat up, groping for his glasses. He put them on and peered in the direction of Morgan's castle. "The Holey Pail didn't say what we were supposed to do once we got to the castle," said Chuckie. "What if Morgan le Fay turns us into statues or something?"

"I know it's kinda scary, Chuckie, but we gotta set my grandpa free," said Tommy. "And then we gotta free Addy's daddy, and the other knights from the dumbgeon. The Holey Pail wouldn't tell us to do something that's impossible. Um, at least, I'm pretty sure it wouldn't. Don't worry. We'll think of something."

The donkeys drew to a halt in front of the castle. The horse knelt so that Tommy could dismount. The drawbridge over the moat was up. Black slimy alligator-like things surfaced and resubmerged in the dark water. Chuckie shivered.

"How do we get into the castle?" whispered Lil. "I don't know how to swim."

"Me either," said Phil, "but even if I could, I don't think I'd want to swim in there." He pointed down into the murky waters.

"Come on, you babies," said Angelica. "I can't come up with every idea around here. How are we gonna get that bridge to come down?"

Tommy thought hard. "I gotta idea!" He began rummaging around in his diaper. He pulled out the golden key that the Babe of the

Bridge had given him. Then he walked over to the edge of the moat.

"Tommy, don't jump!" Chuckie called in an anxious whisper. "You'll get eated by those things!"

Tommy turned around to give Chuckie the thumbs-up sign. Behind him a large, slimy creature that looked like it was part alligator and part eel rose out of the water and opened its jaws, as though expecting Tommy to turn and leap into the moat. Everyone gasped.

But Tommy didn't jump in. He turned back to the moat. The creature closed its jaws and submerged itself partially in the murky water, so that only its eyes protruded above the surface. Tommy held the key in his hand. He had no idea how to make it work. "Hmm," he said to himself. "The Babe of the Bridge said this could open any door, but I don't even see a keyhole or anything." He held the key up before his eyes, then turned it over and over to look at it. He pointed it toward the door across the water, then looked down at the key again. "I wonder if maybe—"

"Look, Tommy!" called Lil.

Tommy looked up. The drawbridge had begun to tremble a little bit. Then slowly, creakily, the drawbridge door began to lower. The key had worked.

They left the donkeys and the cow and the horse and the cart outside. The five of them ran as fast as they could across the drawbridge. Once again they found themselves in the dank entrance hallway. There was no sign of anyone.

"Let's look for my grandpa!" Tommy whispered, tiptoeing over to the doorway into the great hall where he'd last seen him. It was empty.

"Maybe he's down in the dumbgeon," Lil suggested helpfully.

Tommy shuddered. "Let's go check," he said grimly.

They tiptoed across the main hall to where the door to the dungeon stood. Using all their strength they managed to get it open, and this time Tommy led the way down the gloomy stone steps. At the bottom it took a moment for their eyes to adjust to the dim light.

"Gimme that key," hissed Angelica. Tommy handed it to her. Angelica tiptoed forward toward the cell where the knights had been imprisoned. "Hello?" she called.

They heard a scrambling, as though someone was climbing to his feet, and then a voice spoke: "Hark! Who goes there? Be you friend or foe?"

"Hey!" said Angelica. "Are you guys all in there?"

It was Sir Casey who stood at the bars. "Look! It's the child sorceress! We hoped you would return."

"Stand back," said Angelica. She pulled out the key and pointed it at the rusty lock. The door swung inward. A dozen knights in various states of disarray staggered out of the cell.

"Your elfin magic has worked like a charm!" Sir Casey breathed on bended knee. "Our chains sprang open, and the door hath unlocked. Many thanks, child."

"Sure, no problem," said Angelica. "Now, could you tell me where my Grandpa Lou is, and also where my doll is? That is, the rest of my doll?" She pulled out Cynthia's hand and looked at it, and her face clouded with anger.

"The evil Morgan has taken them both, along with her brattish son, to Camelot. She left us here to starve in her dungeon. No one remains but us. The servants have fled in terror. And we prisoners have been without food or water for the two days since we last saw you," said Sir Casey.

"Well, we have plenty of food and a cow right outside," said Angelica cheerfully. She turned to leave. "Come this way!"

Tommy and the others, who had been listening to the conversation, had already climbed back upstairs and hurried outside to their cart and donkeys. "Look!" Tommy whispered to Chuckie, pointing up at the sky. "All the dark clouds floated away. I guess they follow Morgan wherever she goes."

The knights followed Angelica outside the castle. They blinked in the brilliant sunshine.

"There's Addy's daddy!" Chuckie exclaimed.

Phil and Lil handed the knights a basket of food and a pitcher of milk. They gobbled it all down eagerly.

"I'm taking these babies back to the Camel Lot so that we can find our grandpa. You guys want to come along?" said Angelica.

"We shall gratefully follow you back to Camelot," said Sir Nedd. "Just as soon as we retrieve our armor from up in that tree." His expression darkened as he pointed above their heads. Sure enough, bits of armor and shields and visors could be seen hanging from the branches. "Mordred has been doing his magic exercises again."

"Uh, right," said Angelica. "We'll catch ya later."

"Aye, and thanks again for saving us, child sorceress," said Sir Boyle. "We shall meet you at Camelot, and then woe be unto the evil Morgan le Fay. We shall restore the Round Table to its rightful grandeur!"

"I couldn't care less about a dumb table. All I want is my doll!" Angelica said irritably. She and the babies started off again.

"I can't wait to tell Addy her dad is coming back!" said Chuckie.

"I can't wait to see Grandpa!" said Tommy.

"So, Mordred's been practicing his spells, eh?" said Angelica to herself. "Sounds like he's getting worried that he's not the only bully around here! Well, Mordred, you oughta be worried, because here comes Angelica, the great and bee-yoo-tee-ful sorcerless!"

CHAPTER 13

"Are you sure this is the right Camel Lot?" Chuckie whispered, looking around in wonder. "It looks different." The Round Table was full of people playing cards and munching on slices of pizza. Strangely dressed soldiers with French accents milled around.

"It must be!" Tommy whispered back. "But it looks a lot different. I don't see the king and queen or any of the knightses anywhere. And I don't see my grandpa, either."

"Or any of the babies from the nursery," Lil whispered.

"Psssst! Over here!" said a voice behind them.

They turned around quickly. A small figure dressed in a black hooded robe from head to foot was beckoning to them. The figure pulled back the hood ever so slightly to reveal the face beneath.

"Addy!" gasped Chuckie.

Addy put a finger to her lips to silence him, and directed them to follow her into a little broom closet. Once inside with the door closed, Addy threw back her hood. "I'm so glad to see you all safe and sound!" she said. "Did you find out anything about my dad?"

"Yeah, he's on his way here!" said Chuckie.

Addy squealed with delight. Chuckie filled her in on everything that had happened.

"Well, a lot has happened around here, too," Addy said, when Chuckie had finished. "Don't worry, Tommy and Angelica. Your grandpa is safe."

Tommy heaved a sigh of relief.

"So what's going on around here?" Angelica demanded. "Where are all the knightses and King Arthur? And who are all these people walking around dressed up so funny?"

"They're Saxons and Normans, enemies of the king, all working for Morgan. They're helping her try to overthrow King Arthur," Addy replied, shaking her head. "Morgan has been trying to get rid of the king ever since you left. First, she had one of her Saxon archers try to shoot an arrow at him. But he had a deck of your Grandpa's playing cards in his pocket, and the arrow just fell down. Then she had a basket of poisoned apples sent to him. But the first bite got stuck in his new set of false teeth, so he didn't eat any more. And then she tried to hypnotize him but your grandpa's glasses prevented him from focusing on her clearly. So now she's cast a spell over everyone that keeps them asleep until she decides what the best way is to get rid of them all."

"Where are they all sleeping?" asked Phil.

"They're upstairs in the nursery. No one's paid any attention to us babies since all this happened," she added with a little smile. "Morgan told Mordred to get rid of us just like she thinks he got rid of you. He's gonna be in trouble with his mom when she finds out you babies have come back," she added with a devilish giggle.

"Well, what about my grandpa?" asked Tommy.

"Morgan thinks his magic powers are even stronger than hers, so she plans to marry him."

Tommy's and Angelica's mouths fell open. They couldn't believe their ears.

"Mmm-hmmm!" Addy nodded so vigorously, her blond curls bobbed up and down. "She's gone off to buy a bridal dress. That's why she's not here."

"Okay, everybody," Tommy said, turning to the others. "Follow me upstairs! We gotta go wake up the king."

"But, Tommy," Chuckie protested, "Morgan'll probably be back soon!"

"That's right, Chuckie. So we gotta wake the king and the knightses before she tries to turn them into something terrible."

"And we'd better find Grandpa before he marries Morgan le Fay," said Angelica. "That would make Mordred . . . my uncle!" She shuddered. Then she patted a lumpy object in her pocket. "Let's get going."

They climbed up, up, up the winding stone steps until they arrived at the nursery. Tommy was lugging the golden sword, which caused him to walk up the steps backward, heaving it up each step with some difficulty.

They heard the snoring before they had even reached the open doorway. Tommy peered inside.

The room was full of sleeping grown-ups. Angelica and the babies tiptoed among them, stepping over swords and helmets, searching for the king.

"Here he is!" Adelaide called, pointing to a figure draped in scarlet. King Arthur was in a far corner of the nursery. Near him lay Queen Guinevere, slumped across Sir Lancelot.

Still dragging the sword behind him, Tommy staggered over to where Arthur lay. Gently, he swung the hilt of the golden sword around and placed it into the sleeping king's hand. Then he stood up and looked at the others. "We gotta find a way to wake him up! Morgan le Fay will be here any minute!"

Chuckie picked up a horn that was lying on the floor. He gave it a blast. No one stirred.

Lil picked up a pitcher of water and tossed it over the nearest knight. He kept snoring.

Phil picked up a toy hammer and clanged it on the helmet of another knight. A gong-like boom filled the room, but no one moved.

"Hold on a minute," Angelica said, fishing in her pocket. She pulled out a small, sparkly bottle that had an ornate, sparkly stopper in it.

"Hey!" said Tommy. "Isn't that the perfume the maidenses gave to you?"

Angelica nodded. "If this doesn't wake them, nothing will," she said and unstoppered the top.

It didn't take long for the fumes to fill the room. The sleeping knights began to stir, and then cough, sneeze, and rub their eyes.

"Cork that bottle, child! The stench is most vile!" a nearby knight said, coughing.

Everyone began to stagger to their feet.

"Wake up, everyone!" Angelica called. "Morgan le Fay and her annoying son are planning to get rid of you! You'd better do something fast."

King Arthur stood up tall. "To arms, knights!" Then he looked down in surprise at the sword he held in his hand. It glowed with an unearthly brightness in that large, dim room, and all the knights went down on bended knee at the sight of it. "Where did this come from?" he said, holding the sword up before him.

"Oh, that?" said Angelica. "The Holey Pail told us you might want it. We got it over in the field beyond that big lake."

"It looks just like my sword, Excalibur, given to me by the Lady of the Lake when I was a young king, but I thought I'd lost it! Did you say you found it in the lake? Are you . . . the Lady of the Lake, disguised as a rather grubby little child?" Arthur looked at Angelica as though he were seeing her for the first time. "If it be so, then Camelot can be saved!"

"Well, really, Your Highliness, is that any way to talk to a sorcerless?" Angelica said crossly. "If I were you, I would get these knight-ses moving, because Morgan is on her way here to try to cast a nasty spell over you guys. . . ."

"The vulgar little child has spoken the truth," said a voice in the back of the room. Everyone whirled around. There stood Morgan le Fay, holding a battered old book in one hand and a shopping bag from Ye Bonnie Bridals in the other. She stared for a moment at the sword in Arthur's hand, and her lovely brow furrowed into an angry scowl. The sword flew out of Arthur's hand and sailed out the window. They heard a loud CLANK! below in the courtyard.

"What have you done with the sword?" thundered Arthur.

"I've put it safely into a big stone in the courtyard, whence no man may remove it," Morgan said, staring coolly at the king with her ice-green eyes.

"You'll pay for this evil work, Morgan le Fay!" shouted Lancelot.

Morgan rolled her eyes. "Do button up, Lancelot," she said impatiently. "For you have little time left to speak. I have finally found a lovely, evil spell that should take care of the roomful of you." She set down her shopping bag and opened her heavy book of spells. Scanning her finger down the page, she read aloud, "How to make oneself invisible . . . Love potions for the aesthetically challenged . . . How to get rich quick . . . Ah. Here it is," she said delightedly. "How to transform one hundred knights into one hundred nasty little beetles."

Just then Galahad grabbed Morgan's shopping bag and toddled as fast as his chubby little legs would carry him down the side of the room. Morgan raced after him. Just as she reached the middle of the room and was about to grab the bag, Addy, who was stationed across the room near the block table, lifted a block off the toy castle, causing a panel to open directly beneath Morgan's feet.

WHOOOOSH!

With a loud shriek, Morgan disappeared down a slide in the floor. They could hear her furious scream as she traveled all the way down, out into the castle courtyard, in the direction of the moat.

Galahad nudged Tommy. "We've never tried this on a growed-up before," he whispered. "When a baby does it, you only get as far as the courtyard." They heard a loud splash. He grinned at Tommy. "But she made it all the way to the moat!"

The knights in the room had barely had time to react to Morgan's ejection from the room when everyone heard a clattering of hooves outside on the paving stones. Queen Guinevere climbed onto a chair to look out the small window. "The missing knights!" she cried. "They have come back and are driving the Saxons and the Normans from the castle!"

Sure enough, as the knights from the nursery clattered down the stairs, still reeking of perfume, they were greeted by the sight of the dozen knights Tommy and his friends had freed from Morgan's dungeon.

The knights from the nursery joined in the battle below. Sir Boyle, who was fighting valiantly alongside Sir Lancelot, sniffed the air curiously. "Where is that infernal stench coming from, Sir Lancelot?" he called. "It smelleth like perfume!"

"I know not what you are referring to!" Lancelot called back innocently and moved away from his colleague to fight a different clump of Saxons.

"I'm going to go look for Grandpa!" Tommy said to the others, and he crawled away down the hallway, looking in room after room.

"Dum-de-dum," came the sound of singing. Tommy recognized the voice. He hurried along the hallway and peeked into the room. There stood Grandpa Lou, dressed in long, navy blue magician's robes, admiring himself in a mirror.

"Tommy?" said Grandpa Lou. "Is that you? I can't see a cotton-pickin' thing without my glasses!" He walked closer to Tommy. "Why it is you! They told me you'd all gone to the seashore with the royal nannies! Which of course was fine with me, because this is all just a dream, but dagnabit, I've missed you these past coupla days!" He picked up Tommy and carried him out of the room. "You like these duds, do you, sport?" he said, holding out his robe. "I don't have my hearing aid in, but it sounds like everyone's started calling me Merlin. Go figure, eh?"

Downstairs in the courtyard the battle had ended. Panting knights leaned heavily against walls. Others cleaned off their swords. A few others had taken off their spurs and boots and were soaking their feet in the wading pool. Arthur stood in the center of the courtyard,

Grandpa's spectacles still on his nose, survey-
ing the scene.

"Our knights have driven the enemy from
this castle!" Arthur strode over to the side of
the pool. Embedded in the smooth rock was
Excalibur, the golden sword. "I see the sword is
back in the stone. I fear Morgan le Fay's magic
has made it impossible for any man to remove
it, even me, Arthur, King of the Britons."

Grandpa Lou stepped forward. "Nonsense!"
he said, giving Arthur such an encouraging clap
on the back that it sent him reeling forward.
"You did it once; you can do it again!"

Arthur pulled the glasses off his nose and
handed them to Grandpa Lou. "I thank you, sir,
for all that you have done for my kingdom."

Grandpa gratefully accepted his spectacles
back and put them on his nose. "Why, thanks!
It's good to see again!"

"Say good-bye to all that you see before you
now, Arthur," said a steely voice. Everyone
whirled around. There stood Morgan le Fay, her
hair and dress dripping with moat water, her
lips set in a tight line of fury, her face as white

as a sheet. One hand rested on the shoulder of her son, Mordred, who smirked at the crowd and twirled the one-handed Cynthia around by her hair. Morgan's other hand held her book of spells. "You won that battle, but I shall win the war," she said with a cruel smile.

Arthur turned pale.

Morgan raised the book to read the terrible spell.

Grandpa walked over to Morgan and took the book right out of her hands. She stared at him, openmouthed with surprise. "Yessirree," said Grandpa, peering down at the book. "I can even see the fine print! Why, Arthur, you must have polished up these specs for me, because they seem to work better than ever!" Grandpa started to read from Morgan's book:

"*Abracadabra-whistle-tee-beer,*
Make these two people disappear!

"See that?" he said, finishing and turning toward Arthur. "Now all I need is my hearing aid and I'll be right as rain. Why are you all staring like that?" Arthur's jaw had dropped open. Grandpa turned around.

Morgan and Mordred had disappeared in a cloud of orange smoke.

"Cynthia!" Angelica shrieked, racing over to where Mordred had just been. On the ground lay the doll. Angelica plucked the other hand out from the folds of her dress and hurriedly fastened it back on. "She's okay!" Angelica crooned, hugging Cynthia close.

"Adelaide!" called a deep voice from across the courtyard. Sir Nedd of Nutt had just spied his daughter, and he raced over to hug her and cover her with kisses. From over her father's shoulder Addy looked at Chuckie and smiled.

"My horse!" Sir Boyle called as the horse Tommy had been riding clattered into the courtyard. The horse nuzzled the knight warmly.

Arthur strode over to Excalibur, which was still stuck in the flagstone. He took a deep breath and wrapped his two hands around the handle. Then he pulled with all his strength. The crowd gave a collective gasp.

"It moveth not," whispered a knight near Tommy.

Tommy rummaged around inside his diaper and pulled out the key that the Babe of the Bridge had given to him. "Well," he said to himself, "it's worth a try, I guess."

Arthur took another deep breath. He stepped up to the sword.

Tommy pointed the key toward the sword.

Arthur pulled.

The key quivered a bit.

The sword glided effortlessly out of the stone. The crowd cheered.

Arthur turned to Grandpa Lou and the babies. "Thank you, child sorceress," he said to Angelica, "for bringing me my sword and for driving our enemies from the castle."

"And for teaching the royal chef how to make pizza," Sir Lancelot added.

"No problem," said Angelica. "Now as far as repaying me goes, do you think you could have a word with the royal builder? I need him to build me a Superstar Cynthia Beach Bungalow."

As Angelica listed her demands, Arthur

turned to Grandpa Lou. "Sir, we are once again deeply grateful to you for restoring our knights to the Round Table and for sending Morgan away. I ask that you kneel, sir."

Grandpa knelt. Arthur raised his golden sword and tapped Grandpa's shoulders lightly with the flat of it. "With my sword Excalibur I do knight thee, Sir Lou of the Lawn, and grant thee a place by my side at the Round Table. Rise, sir."

Grandpa stood up and beamed at the crowd. He cast off his heavy robes, sat down in his lawn chair, and sighed. "I sure did miss this chair," he said, leaning back and closing his eyes. "Why, I—"

"Look at the sun!" cried one of the knights. "It grows dark!"

Tommy the babies climbed onto the lawn chair close to Lou. Angelica held Cynthia tightly and jumped onto the chair, too.

The world grew pitch-black. And then it began to grow light again.

And just like that, they were all back in the Pickleses' backyard.

140

They heard a screen door slam, and Tommy's parents, Stu and Didi, came out to the backyard with Tommy's little brother, Dil.

"Hi, everyone!" said Didi. "You'll never guess what we found Spike carrying in his mouth out in the front yard?" She held up something blue and plastic and full of holes. "This old, holey pail of Tommy's! Here you go, sweetie," she crooned, kneeling down to hand it to Tommy.

All the babies stared at it.

Grandpa was massaging his temples and looking around in confusion. "I wonder what they put in that iced tea," he muttered to himself. "I think I've had a little too much sun," he went on. Then he stood up and followed Stu and Didi into the house.

"Did it really happen?" whispered Chuckie.

"Of course, Chuckie," said Tommy.

"No way," scoffed Angelica. "Everybody knows that King Arthur and his knightses of the Sand Table is just a story. There's no such thing as the Camel Lot. And there's definitely no such thing as Morgan le Fay or Mordred."

"Then how come we all saw your grandfather

make them disappear?" protested Lil.

"Yeah," said Phil. "I wonder where those two ended up?"

"Angelica!" Didi called, stepping outside. "Your mother just called. She's coming to pick you up soon. She wants you to meet her new colleague, Mrs. LeFeigh. Apparently she has a little boy just your age!"

Angelica looked at Tommy. Tommy looked at Angelica.

"You'd better gimme that stupid pail, Tommy," she said. "I might be needing it."

THE END